This book is for Hugh,

my child of thunder and lightning.

May you find all that is good in life,

with all my love for all time.

Novels in the Djinn Quintet by Linda Davies:

Sea Djinn

Fire Djinn

Look out for Rock Djinn, coming in 2010

Adult novels by Linda Davies

Nest of Vipers

Wilderness of Mirrors

Into the Fire

Something Wild

Final Settlement

These books are for adults,
so your parents might enjoy them!

You can read more about Linda Davies on her website:

www.ex.ac.uk/~RDavies/arian/linda.html
or simply type in lindadavies.com

Praise for Sea Djinn and Fire Djinn by Linda Davies

Media comments

'Dubai's Harry Potter.' Emirates Today

'A joyful fantasy... steeped in the heritage of the region. Wonderful.' Time Out Dubai

Time Out Dubai chose Sea Djinn as the only children's book in its Books of the Year 2007

'A fine piece of prose.' Friday Magazine

'A fast-paced, beautifully descriptive adventure with just the right mixture of compelling characters, well-observed humour and page-turning excitement. The Arabian flavour is perfectly balanced so that the book will appeal to children in Dubai, Arabia and far beyond.' Julia Wheeler

'The author has an amazing feel for words and puts it to effective use.' Khaleej Times

Reader comments

'As a sequel to 'Sea Djinn', 'Fire Djinn' implements a similar plot where we once again see Finn attempt a rescue. Davies' complex and imaginative writing keeps the reader on tenterhooks throughout the book. A must-read for teens - especially those living in Dubai. This adventurous book unveils the challenges of the 'dark world.' Muhammad Ramzanali, 16, English College

'This book is extremely creative and uses a lot of description so you can actually picture the setting in your head as well as what is happening. It made me want to read more and more of it because of the action. I can't wait for Fire Djinn!' Jack, 11, Repton

'I think Sea Djinn is a fantastic book with lots of action and adventure. My Mum and I read this together and we couldn't put it down! I loved the way it was set in Dubai and even knew the road Finn

lived on, so I sort of felt part of the whole story!'
Simon, 11, JESS Arabian Ranches

'I was hooked from the first few pages.'
Dale, 11, Jumeirah Primary School

'A book that unleashes the dangers of the undiscovered world'
Muhammad, 15, English College

'This exciting and innovative story opens the door to a new world. I loved it and look forward to reading Fire Djinn.'
Pauline, 14, English College

'My son and I both loved Sea Djinn. It became a part of our lives when we read it together. We can't wait for Fire Djinn.'
Clare Slater, forty something, London

'Loved it! Sea Djinn is brilliant! Nothing more needs saying, it is simply that good! It has everything a supernatural / fantasy reader needs! Thrills, rides, bit of an epic history plot! But everything in it will keep you reading. The chapters are a fair size, character development is brilliant. I really cared what happened to them from a very early stage...' C. Fisher

'Exciting stuff for the young readers! This is a rattling good tale in the fantasy genre for those about fourteen. Set, unusually, in the Middle East, it tells of a young man, Finn Kennedy, who meets a Sea Djinn Triton, who needs his aid to save the world from his evil counterpart Hydrus. Finn enlists the aid of three other kids in a bid to save the world - and his parents, who have been kidnapped by the evil djinn. It should keep the readers page turning!'
T. Walker (Bedfordshire, UK)

'Sea Djinn is the best book ever! The characters are hysterical and it was fun reading about the same sea that we swim in. Can't wait for Fire Djinn.' Jay, 8, Dubai American Academy

'A breathtaking book which once I started I could not put down. The best book I have ever read.' Berry, 11, Hong Kong Academy

'I loved Fire Djinn because it had so much suspense in it. This book

has so many cliff hangers so I didn't want to put it down. In addition, the imagination for this book was phenomenal. There was lots of action which makes it really enjoyable so I advise anyone to read it. I can't wait for Stone Djinn!'
Jack Morris, Aged 11, Repton Dubai.

'Pls tell Linda that Sasha (10) absolutely DEVOURED Sea Djinn and Fire Djinn. 'Daddy Daddy! I'm on Chapter 7 already and its only the first day!' Frank, Sasha's father.

'Sea Djinn makes you feel as though you are on a long, exciting journey.' Sophie 9, Jumeirah Primary School

'It is a very exciting book. I think it as good as Harry Potter - very nearly better. We couldn't wait to get to the next chapter because it's so good and Linda stops at really exciting places.'
James, 8, Fulham Prep, London

Phenomenal! When Finn meets Triton a sea djinn with super natural powers, his adventures are only beginning. When Finn discovers that his parents have been kidnapped at sea by an evil sea djinn, he has to go on a rescue mission, or maybe not? Will Finn survive? You will have to see for yourself. Mrs. K. Pezet 'book worm' (London)

Great for older kids this is an exciting adventure aimed at older chidlren 11+ or to be read to younger children. This is a really good tale about a young man, Finn Kennedy who meets a Sea Genie who needs help to save the world from an evil tyrant. Very much Arabian Knights stuff and will keep the kids entertained. Worth buying!!
Freespirit 'bo3ss' (UK)

'Magical, adventurous and completely unpredictable'
Tamer, 15, English College

'I did my homework at double quick time every night so that I could be free to read this enthralling book.'
Isobel, 11, Jumeirah Primary School

'Sea Djinn is a fantastic book, and the author holds the reader's interest by making sure there is always something going on. The ending is very clever and entertaining. I found it easy to picture what was happening in my head as the author's imaginative descriptions are very realistic. Sea Djinn is one of the best books I have read this year!' Sarah, 13 Jess Arabian Ranches

'Tia is loving Sea Djinn and I've never known her want to read so much. She has been carrying Sea Djinn around with her and even taking it to school so she can keep reading.'
Lisa, (9 year old Tia's Mum)

'I found the part where Finn dove down under the sea for the pearl to be heart-thumpingly exciting and he was down there for so long I had to take a breath for him!' Garnet, 12, Edmonton Canada

'Both Sea Djinn and Fire Djinn are remarkable. If you start reading, you get trapped inside the book. Also while you're reading the characters come out.' Eunji 10 Jumeirah Primary School

'Sea Djinn is an adventure story about a boy named Finn. I loved reading Sea Djinn because there were great characters and a story line that will leave you wanting to know more.'
Hannah, aged 10, Greenfiled Community School

'Oh to be Finn for just one adventure! Not since my Jennings books in the 60s have I been so magically transported to a place that's would be so fun to be! Pure escapism but so incredibly well written! Can't wait for Stone Djinn.' A critique by your greatest fan
Kevin Dominic Regan, aged 51 ½

'The second of a promising series, 'Fire Djinn' had expectations to live up to; the success of the previous book, 'Sea Djinn', ensured that. Just like her three characters, Fred, Finn and Georgie, Linda Davies was handed a tough task. Nevertheless, she surpassed expectations and 'Fire Djinn' is a triumph.'
'A camping trip in the desert goes very wrong and our three light-fighters stumble upon a palace. Unable to resist, the trio climb aboard a truck which takes them on the road to hell. This series takes you form the shores of Dubai to a magical world far away. Mythical creatures, epic adventures and unimaginable situations; this book has all the right ingredients to spark your interest and set your imagination alight. Book two; two thumbs up.'
Tamer Al Ghussein, 16, English College

STORM DJINN

by

LINDA DAVIES

Fear one thing in all that is....
Fear the Djinn.

The Wishmaster. 1993

CHAPTER ONE

∽ Crash ∽

The Rub al Khali – the Empty Quarter – Abu Dhabi

THE LAND CRUISER BUCKED wildly as it powered across the rough sand. Finn and Georgie whooped with excitement. Fred, face tinged green, groaned softly. He was sure they were going to topple and roll. They were scaling huge dunes, accelerating up them alarmingly fast, then sliding down the other side seemingly out of control. Ahead of them a convoy of cars snaked their way across the burnished sand. The Jumeirah Academy of Music school trip; ten Land Cruisers, thirty pupils, ten teachers and ten drivers.

Finn laid a steadying hand on Fred's arm.

'Relax, we've had bumpier rides than this. Think about the storm when we capsized.'

Fred gave him a pained look. 'Yeah. And what happened to us all after that?'

'Nothing's going to happen,' said Finn. 'We're just going to get a bit sandy, that's all.'

Fred did not look convinced.

'It's all right for you. You're an adrenalin junkie. You have no fear.'

Finn grinned. 'Guilty.'

'Who's an adrenalin junkie?' asked their teacher, Hareb Al Suwaidi, known to all as Hareb. He turned in his seat, draped one elegant arm along the top of it and studied the three of them with narrowed eyes.

Fred and Georgie pointed at Finn.

Hareb nodded. 'Thought as much. We should be in for some fun then,' he observed drily.

They were lucky with him, thought Finn. He was the most well-liked teacher at school, he and Mr Slavel. He was young, in his mid twenties Finn reckoned, an utterly brilliant science teacher and he carried with him a sense of mystery, of the unexplained which intrigued Finn. Whatever he said came out like poetry and he had a deep melodic voice so the effect was mesmerising. Finn noticed that he had replaced his immaculate white kandoora with a dark grey one, looser cut, in a heavy-looking fabric, and he'd changed his white shemargh for a red and white check one.

'Desert gear,' said the teacher with a smile, as if reading Finn's thoughts.

Finn smiled back. 'Tell us about the desert, about the Empty Quarter.'

'The Rub al Khali? It is a beautiful, heartless place where death licks at your heels with every step. Even the Bedu just skirt the flanks, rarely if ever venturing in very deep. Perhaps it is the ultimate test of survivability.' Hareb paused and a wistful look settled in his eyes. 'It's a worthy foe. Most people would die before they got a few miles on foot during high summer. The temperatures reach 55 degrees centigrade, so hot the air sears your nostrils when you breathe. The dunes are taller than the Eiffel Tower. Imagine trying to claw your way up and over them in the blistering heat.'

'Why would anyone want to?' asked Fred.

'Because it's there.' Hareb smiled enigmatically. 'But don't worry, our trip will be just a short escapade.'

'Tame,' murmured Finn to himself.

Hareb heard him and raised a sculpted eyebrow. 'Finn, believe me, tame is what you want in the Rub al Khali.'

'Yes, I suppose it is,' conceded Finn, mind faraway. He gazed out of the window, green eyes sharp with longing.

The dunes of the Empty Quarter stretched out for a quarter of a million square miles around them, a sea of sand, with mountainous waves towering away into the horizon; empty and desolately beautiful. Scary too. They were miles from civilisation, driving back through time it almost seemed, to another age, another millennium where there was just sand and that huge, towering sky curving away to the ends of the earth. No houses. No people. No help. Finn laughed to himself as a flicker of unease rippled through him. Why would they need help? They had ten desert experts driving them, ready to set up their tents for an overnight camp, and all the vehicles were loaded with enough food and water for a week. It was going to be *tame*, he chastised himself.

Finn frowned at the sky and checked his watch; four p.m. - too early to get dark, yet the light was fading. The roar of the Land Cruiser mounting a dune was matched by a louder howl; the wind. Suddenly the atmosphere in the car changed. Finn could feel the tension. He could see it in the veined hands of Shaukat, the driver, as he gripped the steering wheel, and in the hunch of his shoulders.

Fred glanced uneasily out of the window. He saw the sun. It looked odd. It was tinged green, as if burning feverishly. A strange ring of dull brown-grey ran around it, like a dark halo.

'What's happening?' asked Fred, fear churning his stomach.

'A shamal,' answered Shaukat. 'A sandstorm. Coming from nowhere. The sky was blue a minute ago.'

'That's what shamals do,' answered Hareb. 'They come from nowhere. We should stop.'

'As soon as we crest this dune,' replied Shaukat. 'If we stop here, we'll get stuck in the sand.'

Finn glanced at his teacher. Hareb's voice had sounded oddly ominous. But then he was an Emirati, he had grown up in the Liwa Oasis on the edge of the Empty Quarter, so he would know better than any of them what a shamal could do.

Suddenly, Hareb flinched as though in pain. Finn watched him, concerned.

Sand wheeled through the air and pummelled the car windows as if it were trying to break in. Finn wondered how the driver could see to drive, yet the car powered on, racing upwards towards the top of some hidden dune. Finn tried to spot the other cars ahead, but there was no sign of them. Perhaps they had already crested the dune and were down on the other side.

Atop the dune, the car shuddered as a gust hit it full blast. Shaukat gasped as the car began to angle up on two wheels. Fred gulped, Georgie turned white and Hareb glanced round, face tight with apprehension.

'Hang on!' he shouted. 'Brace yourselves!'

Sickeningly and seemingly in slow motion, the car toppled. It rolled one eighty degrees, suspending them in the air before tipping the whole way over and thudding down again. Finn covered his head with his hands, like air hostesses show you to do in the safety demonstrations on planes. He held his breath as the car rolled again, then again, then again, picking up speed as it went, like a demented fairground ride, only there was no getting off *this* ride. The screams were real, the danger was mortal and they were trapped. The wind screamed back at them. Darkness fell, devouring the light.

CHAPTER TWO

∽ Fireball ∾

T HE CAR'S ENGINE TICKED over but its wheels spun impotently in the air. Finn's eyes flicked open. Upside down, hanging upside down, the taste of blood in his mouth, blood blurring his already unsteady vision. He rubbed his eyes savagely, glanced around; Georgie, Fred, Shaukat and Hareb were all hanging upside down and unconscious. *Unconscious, that was all,* he prayed violently. *Not dead. Not dead.*

Finn struggled to unclick his seat belt which was jammed hard into his chest. As he battled with it, the roaring wind carried the scent of petrol to him. His mind raced; *ruptured petrol tanks, a hot car, risk of explosion.* Desperately, he fumbled with the seat belt, finally getting it undone. He stuck out his hands, braced himself and fell to the car's ceiling. He grappled with Georgie's seat belt and caught her as she fell. He laid her down beside him and tried to open the door. Jammed. He yanked at the handle, kicked at the door, finally it yielded and fell open. Finn grabbed hold of Georgie and dragged her out onto the sand. The wind seemed to battle him as he struggled to drag his cousin away from the car. Step, drag, breathe; step, drag, breathe as the wind pummelled on. Five, ten, fifteen, twenty agonisingly slow feet away. Finn roared back at the wind in fury and frustration, felt a new strength surge through him, and hauled Georgie another twenty feet from the car. Not sure if that was far enough but he had to get the others. Fred next. Seatbelt stuck. Finn struggled, but it refused to release. The smell of fuel grew stronger. Finn grabbed his backpack, took out his Swiss Army knife and cut through the seatbelt, caught Fred and with his new surge of strength, dragged him out onto the sand, over to where Georgie lay prone.

The wind screamed with a savagery almost human. Fear thudding in his chest, Finn ran back, opened the front passenger door and released Hareb, who was groaning now, slowly recovering consciousness.

'C'mon,' screamed Finn. 'We have to get away from the car before it explodes.'

Hareb's eyes flew open. He staggered with Finn out onto the sand. Finn raced round to the other side and hauled at Shaukat's seat belt. He unclicked it. Shaukat fell heavily onto Finn, who could not hold his weight. Finn screamed for Hareb to help, and the teacher staggered round the car and pulled Shaukat off him and dragged him out. Finn rushed out after him and together they pulled Shaukat up to where Georgie and Fred were still lying motionless. Finn rushed back to the car, grabbed his backpack and sprinted back to the others.

He bent over Georgie's chest to check for breathing. As he did so, an explosion ripped through the air as the Land Cruiser's petrol tanks blew. He and Hareb were flung backwards. They lay gasping for breath as flames shot into the sky. A fireball fifty feet high. Like a sign. Like Jehannem, the Dark Fire Djinn, thought Finn with a wave of sickness as the flame scorched his face.

He battled the thought. No. The fireball was good. The other cars would see it, even through the driving sand which made everything more than five feet away invisible. They *had* to see it and come back and rescue them. If they didn't they would be stranded in the vastness of the Empty Quarter. Finn's own thoughts came back to him: *miles from civilisation, no houses, no people, no help.*

CHAPTER THREE

Something's Coming

GEORGIE MOANED SOFTLY. SHE opened her eyes and gazed round in horror.

'Oh my God,' she mouthed.

Finn squeezed her hand, relief coursing through his veins, then he bent over Fred. He could see Fred's chest rising and falling, but his friend seemed to be deeply unconscious.

'Fred, Fred, wake up!' Finn urged, rubbing his hands. Fred lay inert. Finn eyed the large welt where Fred's forehead must have smashed into the car's side window. He kept rubbing Fred's hands. Georgie pushed herself up and struggled over to Fred. She bent double with the effort. The shamal was so strong it was almost impossible to make any headway against it. She slumped down by his body.

'Fred!' she shouted. 'Wake up. Wake up Fred!'

Abruptly Fred's eyes flew open and he gazed about wildly. 'Wh-What? Ohmigod.'

'We need to move,' muttered Hareb. 'It's coming. I know it's coming. I can feel it. We *have* to find somewhere to hide, we-' the wind screamed again and stole his words. Finn and Georgie exchanged a look. Hareb must be concussed.

Suddenly Shaukat woke up. He struggled to his feet.

'Are you OK?' he yelled, eyes taking in the scene. 'The car!' he spread his hands through the acrid smoke that was still pumping from the blazing car.

'Help. We must get help.' He fumbled in his pocket for his mobile. 'No signal,' he shouted. 'Stay here, all of you. Do not move. I am going to climb to the top of the dune to get a signal. I'll be back in fifteen minutes, max.'

Finn watched him battling away through the wind and up the dune, scrambling on all fours. Hareb shouted after him: 'It's out there, searching. *Come back!*'

'Stay with the children,' shouted Shaukat. 'I'll be back soon.'

Finn, Fred and Georgie huddled together, closing their eyes against the sand that lashed into them, scouring any exposed skin. The wind seemed to be increasing in speed. Finn had only ever once heard a wind like this, in Fred's boat, in the Sea of Storms, when Hydrus was chasing them.

Hareb crouched down beside him. 'It's coming,' he mouthed. 'We must hide. *Please, believe me,*' he shouted, eyes wide with terror.

CHAPTER FOUR

❧ Disappearance ❧

THE SECONDS TICKED BY into minutes but Shaukat did not return. The Shamal worsened. Breathing became a struggle. The wind lashed into them, forcing the breath from their lungs. The sand-strafed air, clouded with acrid, black smoke from the burning car filled their mouths. They hunched together, eyes shut, holding hands and waiting. Hareb had taken off his shemargh and spread it across their heads, but it gave scant shelter. Finn prayed that Shaukat would return soon, bringing help with him. The other cars must be somewhere near. If they could just get to them.

Finn glanced at his watch. Twenty minutes had passed. Shaukat had promised to be back in under fifteen. He glanced at Hareb. The teacher seemed to be in pain. His face was contorted.

Finn watched five more minutes tick by, but still the driver did not return. He let go of Georgie's hand and pulled his mobile from his pocket. The wind was so strong that it threatened to rip the phone from his fingers. No signal. He inched across the sand to Hareb.

'Shaukat's disappeared!' he screamed. 'He should have been back by now.'

'It's found him,' Hareb mouthed to himself. He turned to Finn. 'Shaukat's gone,' he shouted. 'It's just us now. We have to hide.'

Suddenly he grabbed his head with both hands and moaned with pain.

'Are you all right?' shouted Finn. 'Are you concussed?' That would account for his ramblings, thought Finn.

'Finn, listen to me. We have to get away from here. The car is a marker.'

Finn stared at Hareb. For all the madness of his words, he did not look concussed. He looked terrified, but quite lucid.

'Come, we *must* go,' the teacher urged.

Finn inched back to Georgie and Fred. A blood-curdling scream ripped through the air. It could have been human, or it could have been the wind. Finn felt something then, a blackness, a dragging feeling, like a magnet, pulling at him. The wind pummelled his body one way, and this force seemed to pull it the other. He glanced across at his teacher's desperate face.

'Come! Now!' roared Hareb, stretching out his hand.

Shaukat had cautioned them against moving. He had insisted they stay put. If he were coming with help and they moved, how would he find them? All these questions raged in Finn's head, but still he saw the unveiled terror in his teacher's eyes, felt the force pulling him, growing stronger.

Another scream ripped through the air, louder than the roaring wind. Fred and Georgie glanced at Finn, their own eyes wide with terror. Finn made up his mind.

'C'mon!' he yelled to Fred and Georgie. 'Let's move.'

They scrambled to their feet. The wind punched them and they fell to their knees. They stayed on all fours, crawling forward in the direction the wind was pushing them. Finn, despite the power of the wind behind him, felt like he was dragging a huge weight. So, he noticed, did Hareb. He was straining to move, sweat slicking down his face.

The wind grew stronger still. Georgie felt as if it were trying to rip her limbs from her body. There seemed to be hatred in its savagery. The sand blinded them. All they could do was just put one hand before the next and crawl onwards, away from the car, away from the sense of danger and horror that stalked them.

Suddenly, Hareb collapsed on the sand, grabbing his head again. Finn bent over him. His teacher's eyes were clamped shut with pain.

'Go!' Hareb shouted. 'It wants me. Just go as far away as you can, away from me. It'll leave you alone if it has me.'

'What?' screamed Finn. 'What are you talking about?'

Hareb opened his eyes and looked hard into Finn's. 'Tell them, at the lab. In Boston. In the US. Mark Hayward. Tell him it got me.'

'Nothing's got you!' shouted Finn.

'It *is* getting me. I'll be dead in minutes.'

Finn searched Hareb's eyes for insanity, found none, just saw fear and a great sadness and the unmistakeable intensity of truth.

'Who?' shouted Finn. 'Tell me who?'

His teacher slumped back on the sand. Finn could see him struggling to speak. He opened his mouth, Finn stuck his ear next to it to hear the faltering voice, but then, abruptly, the teacher's eyes closed and all the life seemed to go out of him.

Finn let out a roar of rage. 'Nooooo!' he screamed. 'You will not die here. You will not.'

Chapter Five

⨍ Mirage ⨍

FINN BENT HIS HEAD to Hareb's chest. His teacher was still breathing, but faintly, and his heartbeat was weak and seemed to be slowing. Finn summoned his powers. He felt the strength surge through him in response and he hauled Hareb onto his own back. Something was killing his teacher, perhaps just pure fear, but whatever it was, Finn had to get him away from it.

He glanced across at Fred and Georgie. 'You all right?' he shouted. They nodded, eyes wide with fear.

'Let's move,' shouted Finn. Inch by inch, foot by foot, he crawled forward, dragging his teacher on his back. The force still pulled at him, seemingly trying to stop him. He gave a shout of rage and effort and fought it with every ounce of his strength. Sweat poured off him and he was soon trembling with effort. His muscles burned and his eyes felt the lacerations of a million grains of sand blinding him. He struggled to see something, to see *anything* in the maelstrom of sand. Perhaps a car, come to rescue them. Perhaps Shaukat coming back to them, maybe just a tree or a bush behind which they could shelter.

His eyes streamed profusely. Through the blur he thought he saw a hand, reaching out to them. Great. Now he was hallucinating. He shook his head and crawled on. The force pulling at him was growing stronger. Progress of any sort was almost impossible. He would move forward, pushed by the wind, but then the force would drag him back. They must be in a whirlwind, Finn reckoned. Would they be sucked up into the furious air, blown across the Empty Quarter, dropped from the sky a hundred miles away? Finn rubbed his eyes. There it was again, a brown hand reaching out through a wall of sand.

The wind shrieked its inhuman lament. Finn could feel the evil in the tormented air, in the force dragging him backwards, hunting him.

The hand gestured, frantically this time. Finn turned to Fred and Georgie. They were staring in disbelief at the hand.

'It's a mirage,' screamed Georgie. 'We're seeing things, Finn.'

Finn glanced back over his shoulder. He could see nothing behind, just the sand-filled hell.

'Come!' urged a voice seemingly from behind the wall of sand. 'Quick. He's nearly upon us.'

'Mirages do not speak!' yelled Finn, eyes pleading with Georgie and Fred. He took another instant decision. The hand was not the source of the evil that swirled around them in the screaming air. He reached out his own hand and clasped the outstretched brown one.

'Hold on to each other,' urged the voice.

Georgie hesitated for a second, then she grabbed hold of Finn's free hand. Fred grabbed Georgie's hand. They felt an enormous yank, a great squeezing, and then the roar of silence.

CHAPTER SIX

∽ Shamal ∽

THEY FOUND THEMSELVES LYING in a heap in a room. Of the hand that had beckoned them, there was no sign. The light was muted. Candles flickered. Walls were covered with dark red curtains stirring in a seemingly source-less breeze, revealing brilliant flashes as if the walls were made of gold. The floor was covered wall to wall with a profusion of overlapping rugs, soft and silky.

Finn felt the weight of his teacher on his back. He carefully rolled Hareb onto the floor and bent over his prone body. He felt for a heartbeat, frantically moving his hand over the man's chest. Finally, he found it. Pump…pump… pump…so slow, so faint, but there.

'He's alive. Just.'

Georgie bent over Hareb and took his hands in hers.

'He's cold!' she exclaimed. 'So cold.' She began to rub his hands.

Fred dug into his pocket. He pulled out a small, smooth grey stone.

'Vulcan's Fire Stone. Maybe it'll work on him,' he said, prising open Hareb's hand and closing it around the stone. 'Vulcan said his fire stones would warm us if we were cold, cool us if we were hot, burn us if a Dark Fire Djinn were near. Let's hope we can heal others with them too.'

'Good idea,' said Finn. He unzipped a pocket and pulled out his stone, putting it in Hareb's other hand, while Georgie pulled hers from her pocket and placed it over Hareb's heart.

All three stared at their teacher, lying prone, hovering on the brink of death, and prayed.

'Heal him, please Vulcan, in the name of LightFighters,' intoned Georgie, eyes shut, mind back on Shell Beach where Vulcan, the Fire Djinn of the Light, had presented them with his stones.

The stone lying on the teacher's chest began to glow, first a faint orange, then with strands of gold and blue shimmering through it like flames. Georgie reached over and touched the stone.

'Feel it!' she whispered.

'It's warm!' exclaimed Fred.

'Let's hope it's not too late,' said Finn, seeing the pallor unchanged on Hareb's face. He pulled some of the smaller silk rugs over the inert body of his teacher. As he did so, he exposed gaps between the rugs. Gaps which revealed a shimmering golden floor.

'Where are we?' mouthed Georgie, in a voice trapped between fear and awe.

A movement distracted them. In the furthest, darkest corner of the room, the air seemed to thicken. There was a shimmering, viscous quality to it as if it were liquid. Finn, Fred and Georgie watched it, transfixed.

A hand, a brown hand, an arm, a leg, a body, a matching set of limbs, and lastly a face materialised across the room before their blinking eyes. A boy about their age. He wore a dark brown kandoora and his head was swathed with a black and white shemargh, Bedu-style. He was wiry-looking, fine boned, but there was an aura of great strength about him. His face was elfin, sculpturally handsome. His looks and the tilt of his chin gave him an aristocratic air. The boy smiled at them.

'He should be better now,' he said, rolling his r in accented but perfect English, nodding towards Hareb.

'He'll come round in a couple of minutes,' he added.

Finn studied the boy. He had faraway eyes that gleamed with the light of adventure, but they were tinged too with sorrow as if they had seen too much of the world and its cruelty. Finn knew that look. He saw it in the mirror every day.

'Who are you?' he asked. 'Where are we? And what on earth was going on out there?'

The boy laughed. 'So many questions.' He padded lightly across to them and squatted down beside Hareb. He picked up the fire stone from Hareb's chest. 'It's warm!' he exclaimed.

Georgie held her hand out for the stone. The boy seemed to think for a while before handing it to her. Georgie pocketed it quickly.

'I think you'd better tell me who you four are, and why he is hunting you,' said the boy.

'Who is hunting us?' broke in Finn.

'My questions first,' replied the boy, with a touch of steel in his voice.

Finn, Fred and Georgie fell silent, each studying him. There was something unreadable about him. He was no ordinary boy, that much was certain. He had saved them, brought them out of the storm. He had Power, they could all feel that. *But who was he? Could they trust him?*

Georgie followed her instincts. There was goodness in him. She was sure of it. She broke the silence. 'We are Finn, Georgie and Fred,' she replied. 'And that is our teacher, Hareb.'

'We're on a school trip,' said Fred. 'The sky was blue, then this storm came out of nowhere. Our car rolled. Finn got us out just before the car blew up.'

'Then he nearly died,' said Finn, pointing to Hareb. 'Like you, he was talking about someone hunting us.'

Hareb's eyes fluttered open.

'We're dead,' he said in a voice full of wonderment. Slowly, grimacing with pain, he sat up. 'But this doesn't look like paradise.' The fire stones clattered out of his hands. Georgie scooted forward and gathered them up, quickly handing Finn and Fred theirs.

The boy watched her, eyes curious. He turned back to the teacher. 'You're not dead,' he said with a slight smile. 'Not yet anyway. And this is not paradise, though it is my home.' He bowed formally to them all.

'I am Shamal,' he said. 'And this is the Kingdom of Air.'

CHAPTER SEVEN

∽ Typhon ∽

INN, GEORGIE AND FRED looked at each other in amazement. *'The Kingdom of Air?'* mouthed Georgie. Finn turned to gaze at Shamal. Was he a djinn? An Air Djinn?

Hareb rubbed his head. He must be concussed, hearing things.

'Wherever we are, whatever hallucinations I might be having, it's not safe for any of you here with me,' he said urgently. 'It'll track me.'

The boy shook his head.

'He can track no-one in here.'

'Why are you so sure?' asked Hareb.

'I'll tell you. We will talk. But first you must refresh yourselves. Mrs Constance,' Shamal said to the air, 'refreshments, light if you please, in the Safe Room. No, in my house, not my father's. For five. Oh, and some extra towels too please.' He waited a minute or so, then rose to his feet, crossed the room and drew back one of the curtains to reveal another room, much smaller, similarly curtained. Georgie, Fred and Finn, questions burning in their eyes, followed him.

A table stood at the far end of the room. Gleaming atop the dark wood were two golden jugs, five golden goblets and a golden bowl, full of fruit. There was also, incongruously, a pile of towels.

'Who's Mrs Constance?' whispered Fred. 'How'd she get in?'

'And out?' added Finn.

Shamal, seemingly gifted with acute hearing, turned to them. 'Mrs Constance is an evolved human, who happens to share some of our aims. She helps where she is needed.'

He picked up one of the golden jugs and poured out water for all of them as they pondered his words. Fred wondered if he were an evolved human, or just a bog standard un-evolved one.

'This place is like Aladdin's cave,' said Georgie.

Shamal smiled. 'I'm not exactly sure of the provenance, but I think these pieces *might* have come from Aladdin's cave. We'll have to ask my father.'

Georgie flicked a glance at Fred as if to say, *is he serious?*

Fred shrugged. He took the goblet Shamal handed him, sniffed cautiously at the water, then drained it. He discreetly turned the goblet this way and that, letting the candle light fall on what looked like ancient runes, worn faint by time and handling.

'Perhaps you'd like to freshen up a bit,' said Shamal. 'There's a bathroom through there,' he indicated a heavily carved wooden door.

They filed through, while Hareb stayed behind with Shamal. Georgie gulped when she saw her face in the mirror. There was a big bruise flowering across her cheek, and her auburn hair, normally extravagantly wavy flew off from her face as if still propelled by the wind. She tried to run her hands through it and gave up. 'Urgh,' she complained, 'it's thick with sand.'

Fred grinned, 'Whereas Finn and I look just peachy.'

Georgie giggled. Fred's short black hair stood on end too, making him look as if he had been hit by lightning. He also had a huge angry-looking bump on his forehead. While Finn's face was streaked with blood and his jaw-length, sun-bleached surfer hair was matted with more blood. Finn cleaned up his face, but there wasn't much he could do for his hair.

'What d'you think of Shamal?' whispered Georgie.

'He's quite something, isn't he?' mused Finn. 'He has Power, you can feel it, but he seems too young to be an Air Djinn, and besides he looks quite human.'

'So did Jehannem, when he wanted to,' observed Fred, 'and who says Djinn can't be children? It's just that we haven't met young ones, but they must exist.'

'True,' admitted Finn. 'What or who exactly, he is, I don't know.'

'He talks like someone much older, don't you think?' asked Georgie.

'Chock full of secrets, that's for sure,' observed Fred.

The other two nodded.

'Let's go and see what we can find out,' said Finn, 'and then work out how the heck to get back out of the Kingdom of Air and find the rest of the JAM guys. I'm worried about them, not to mention Shaukat.'

They rejoined Shamal who was talking in Arabic with Hareb. He turned to them with a smile.

'Please, take some fruit,' he urged. Under the guise of hospitality, he studied them. The tallest one, Finn, had an aquiline, almost regal nose and sharp green eyes dancing with secrets. Shamal could feel the Power pulsing from him like a heat source. Who are you? wondered Shamal. *Could you be? Could you be?* He turned his attention to the other boy, Fred. He had keen, intelligent eyes and emitted a feeling of quiet confidence, as if he had seen some of the worst that the world could throw at him and weathered it. While the girl, Georgie, with her mischievous, elfin face and wild hair, radiated a kind of valiant courage. Then there were those strange, hot stones which seemed to have Power of their own. They were LightFighters, he was sure of it.

'Come through,' he said as they finished their fruit. He led them back into the room of carpets where he sank gracefully to the ground and sat cross-legged, straight-backed. Finn, Fred, Georgie and Hareb sat in a semi circle opposite him.

The candlelight danced in the breeze. The smell of incense drifted through the red-curtained room, rich, beguiling, intoxicating. Georgie breathed in the fragrant air and felt herself strangely calmed. Shamal's voice with its soft cadences, its glorious rolling rs, seemed to mesmerise her.

'Now that we are all refreshed and a little stronger, we can talk. What do you know about who was chasing you?' Shamal asked Hareb.

'It is a long story.'

'I have all the time in the world.'

Hareb gazed at the billowing curtains. He blew out a long, slow breath. He flicked his eyes from face to face and then he began to speak.

'It started when I was at Graduate school in the States. I had already done my undergrad in Nuclear Physics, and I was doing my PhD on the subject of parallel universes and time. I worked with two partners, a Dane called Axel Johansen and a Brit called Mark Hayward. We worked on Dark Matter and Anti Matter, Black Holes and unaccounted for spaces and times in the universe.' Hareb's eyes snapped back to the present. 'We were going to write a paper, but then things started happening.'

'What things?' asked Finn.

'We'd come into the lab in the mornings and find our computers had been wiped clean. Totally clean. Everything gone. So we backed everything up and I stored copies in a bank vault. We worked on laptops and took them home every evening. Then Axel had his laptop wiped clean at home. A week later he was driving on an empty road on a sunny day at noon when he drove straight into a tree at 100 kilometres per hour. The police said no other car was on that stretch of road. They could find no reason at all for him to crash.'

'But he did crash,' said Finn.

'Yes. At his funeral I felt as though I were being watched. Couldn't shake that feeling, wherever I went. I knew his death had something to do with our work, so I redoubled my efforts. I wanted to find out everything.' He paused and a flash of anger burned through his eyes. 'I thought at first it was some dubious US government agency that was after us, but the more work I did, the more I sensed it was something else.' He paused, barked out a laugh. 'Look, I'm a scientist, a rationalist, but I became convinced that what was shadowing me, what had killed Axel was something not quite human. Something alive with a hideous dark energy all of its own.'

Shamal's face was sombre. 'You are right. It was. It is.'

'*What* is it?' asked Finn, eyes burning with curiosity.

'The Dark Storm Djinn, Typhon. Otherwise known as the Dark Wind, or Dark Matter.'

Chapter Eight

❧ Why Me? ❧

F RED GULPED. GEORGIE LET out a cry. Finn felt himself reeling. Another Dark Djinn. He'd known it, down in his subconscious. He had felt the evil and the Power as he was being hunted. Hareb had said that 'it', Typhon, was after him, but Finn felt sure that Typhon had been after him too.

'Dark Storm Djinn?' Hareb rubbed his head again. He wasn't hearing this. Any of this. He must be unconscious, dreaming it all. Well, he might as well pursue the dream, or the nightmare, rather.

'Why does this *Dark Storm Djinn* chase me?' demanded Hareb. 'What am I to him? And for that matter, what on earth is a Storm Djinn, Dark or Light?' Hareb got up and began to pace. 'I'm an Emirati!' he declared, flinging his arms wide. 'I was brought up on tales of djinn. *Be a good boy or the djinn will get you,* well you know, never in my wildest nightmares did I think I would *actually* meet one, or be hunted by one. I'm beginning to think that I must have been a very bad boy.'

Shamal smiled. 'No, not a bad boy. A threat.'

'A threat?' railed Hareb. 'Me? How can I be a threat to a Dark Djinn?'

'I think it is time you met my father,' announced Shamal.

CHAPTER NINE

The Dark Meniscus

S HAMAL GAZED OUT ACROSS the endless sands, then he glanced up at the sun.

'Good. He has gone for now. Back to the Dark Kingdom.'

'How can you be sure?' asked Hareb.

'The Dark Meniscus has gone.'

'What the heck is a Dark Meniscus?' asked Georgie.

'A dark circle which surrounds the sun or the moon,' replied Shamal.

'I saw it earlier!' exclaimed Fred. 'When we were driving. It was like an enormous dull brown-grey halo of light that circled the sun, with a darker line at its outer borders.'

'It is Typhon's sign,' proclaimed Shamal. 'It appears around the sun or moon whenever he enters or leaves his own kingdom. It is traces of his Dark Matter. It is the stain of evil, of darkness he leaves on your sky. It's safe to move now. Come on.'

Shamal drew his arms back and forth before the curtained wall, quietly incanting strange and musical words. With a quiet hiss, the wall drew back. Before them stretched a road, perhaps twelve feet wide, suspended in the air, made of cobbles of a pale sandstone colour, vaguely transparent, like amber. Below the road, many hundreds of feet below, reckoned Fred, gazing down apprehensively, was the desert.

Shamal turned to them with a smile. 'Shall we?'

Four pairs of eyes glanced at the huge drop beneath the floating road and swallowed nervously. But they nodded, fascination vying with fear.

Shamal led the way. Georgie went next, edgily suspending her foot above the floating road for a moment, then gingerly adding weight, half suspecting that the cobble would shift under her foot. It held firm, as she knew it must, watching Shamal stride on ahead of her. But then the manner of his appearance, materialising from air, and his very name suggested he was ethereal, not quite solid.

Fred went next, then Finn and finally, Hareb, who tried valiantly not to look down.

They walked in single file through the sky. After a few minutes a structure became visible in the distance, shimmering like a mirage. Finn rubbed his eyes, but the image remained. Perhaps a quarter of a mile away, a castle rose up in the air. With high, battlement-topped walls, towers and minarets it looked like something out of a Thousand and One Nights. It seemed to be built of the same amber-like sandstone as the road. It was unimaginably beautiful.

Shamal turned and bowed to them. 'My father's home; the Castle of the Winds.'

'Can't it be seen from the desert?' asked Georgie, staring at it in wonder.

'This is the Empty Quarter,' replied Shamal. 'Few people come through here. If you looked up you might see the vague outlines. Some people do. They call it a mirage!'

Hareb turned to look at them. 'Some people say mirages are real, that they are shimmering images of actual places hidden beyond the curvature of the earth.'

'What do you think?' Georgie asked him.

He gave her a rueful smile. 'I would have to answer, after my experiences of the last few months, that anything is possible!'

CHAPTER TEN

Zephyr and the Castle of the Winds

A S THEY NEARED THE castle they saw an enormous wooden door, a hundred feet high, barring their way. Shamal paused before it. He raised his head and let out a sound, half cry, half song in the same lilting language he had spoken in before. With a whisper the door swung open.

They walked into a huge, deserted courtyard. Tall palm trees reached majestically towards the skies. Fountains danced in the centre of a large, azure pool. Birds with dazzling green and violet plumage bathed their fluttering wings in the water. Other than the birds, there was no sign of life. An enormous brazier stood behind the fountain. Tendrils of smoke billowed from it, stirred by a gentle breeze, filling the air with the heady scent of incense.

Finn stiffened, aware of a presence. The air around him stirred and shimmered. He felt himself being scrutinised.

'Who's there?' he asked quickly.

Georgie and Fred froze and gazed worriedly at Finn. Hareb stood tall, watchful and wary.

A warm breeze caressed their cheeks like a giant breath. Through the air drifted words, close, low and enduring, molten like honey running over rock.

'I am known by many names. You never see me, but you hear me in the chattering of palm fronds, in the rattling of boats' halyards, you feel me on your face, brushing past on my way somewhere, anywhere the wind blows. I fill the sails, speed the boats on their way, turn the turbines that attempt to capture my power. My absence is death. My absence is a boat becalmed in the doldrums, no wind to fill her sails, men dying of thirst. I am the restless moaning you hear at night when a storm batters your home and blows away evil. Everyone knows me. Or thinks they do…..They call me Santa Ana, they call me Chinook, they have a hundred names for me. I am Zephyr, Djinn of the Winds.'

As the voice spoke, the palm fronds rattled, hidden grass whispered, the high battlements moaned, the heady perfume of distant flowers drifted through the warm air.

The wind faded and the voice echoed away. The children and Hareb stood transfixed. That voice, thought Georgie. She could have listened to it forever. It seemed to carry the whole of the world in it.

It was silent now, waiting. Finn bowed deeply.

'I am Finn,' he said, solemnly. The wind flowed around him. He could discern the intellect reading him, brilliant like a diamond.

Georgie bowed as the wind streamed on to her. 'I am Georgie.' She felt warmth, like a father's love and a great compassion ebb into her.

'I am Fred,' said Fred, bowing in turn, bathed in warmth and understanding as a mind probed his.

'And I am Hareb,' announced Hareb, with a formal bow. 'I am their teacher.' There was a frisson in the wind. Far away, there was a rumble of thunder. It rattled through the battlements and died away.

They all shivered.

The wind danced around them. Warm, protective.

'Welcome to the Castle of the Winds,' said Zephyr.

Shamal smiled as it caressed his face.

'Welcome son of mine,' it intoned, 'light of my eyes, joy of my years.'

'Thank you, Father,' said Shamal, closing his eyes and reaching out his arms to embrace the wind. For a while, the boy just stood, encircled by the wind, a poignant almost pained joy radiating from his face.

Finn, Georgie and Fred watched, warmed by the love they saw before them. They exchanged a look. Now they knew who and what Shamal was. The son of a Djinn Lord.

Shamal opened his eyes. 'May we sit, Father? These travellers are tired. They have had an encounter with Typhon.'

'I saw his mark. You saved them.'

Shamal nodded. 'They have stories to tell Father, stories I know, and stories that shimmer unspoken in their eyes.'

There was a whooshing sound and a carpet appeared, flying towards them. It slowed to a stop before them and hovered about two feet in the air, gently undulating.

'Hop on,' said Shamal.

'A flying carpet!' exclaimed Georgie, not quite believing her own eyes.

Shamal smiled. 'This part of the world is famous for them. But the carpets themselves have no power. It is my father who flies them.'

'Er, of course,' said Georgie, grinning enormously as she scrambled on. Fred jumped on beside her, chuckling in amazement and wobbling precariously. Somewhat cautiously, Hareb alighted.

Finn hopped on and stood for a few moments, swaying on the hovering carpet as if he were riding a wave on his surfboard. He crossed his ankles and sank down.

With the ease of habit, Shamal stepped onto the carpet and elegantly sat, cross-legged. They all gazed for a moment at the birds that had taken off and now wheeled and played between the towers and minarets, chasing each other with raucous shrieks, like air-bound children playing tag.

Hareb cleared his throat. 'Er, Zephyr, Djinn Lord. I assume that if Typhon is the Dark Storm Djinn, that you are the Storm Djinn of the Light?'

'Correct.'

'Good. That's a relief,' Hareb remarked drily. 'I seem, amazingly,' he glanced at Finn, Fred and Georgie, 'to be the only person with this question, but what exactly is a Djinn, particularly a Storm Djinn? I've heard tales as a boy, but they never conjured anything like you. More like Aladdin with his genie in the lamp.'

There was a low, molten chuckle. 'Aladdin did have his genie, but we are a bit different. We have existed since the beginning of time, the myriad of lower Djinn, and the Djinn Lords. We are created from smokeless fire. We occupy a high place in the pantheon of power, below Archangels but above demons. We can be good and we can be evil, rather like you humans. But unlike humans, we can transform or shape shift between various forms, like stones, rivers, fire, water, the wind and we can veil ourselves as animals. The bigger the animal the more powerful the Djinn. The most powerful Djinns, the Djinn Lords, can and often do assume human form.'

'Jehannem,' mouthed Georgie to Finn and Fred. They nodded discreetly.

'How long do Djinn Lords normally live?' continued Hareb.

'Thousands of years,' hummed Zephyr, his voice rich with wonder. 'Unless we sicken or are killed in battle.'

'Don't take this the wrong way,' said Hareb. 'But how could you be killed? I mean how can you kill the wind?'

Zephyr gave a low rolling chuckle, like the burbling of a river. 'There are ways. You will forgive me if I do not spell out the recipe for my own death. It is not a message I wish to send out into the ether.'

'Understood,' replied Hareb, 'but what do you do with all that *time*? What is your role?' he asked, face avid with curiosity.

'Simply to rule our Kingdoms in peace. At least that is the wish of the Djinn Lords of the Light. But the Djinn Lords of the Night, they want power above all else. They want to conquer our dominions, which we are destined to rule over jointly.'

Hareb nodded. 'Fascinating. But why is Typhon, the Dark Storm Djinn, interested in me? Your son Shamal says it is because I am threat to him. But how on earth can I, a mere human, a science teacher, be a threat to him?'

'Because you have power,' answered Zephyr, 'and because of the Prophecy.'

CHAPTER ELEVEN

The Prince
of Atlantis

'WHAT PROPHECY?' ASKED HAREB, voice low
with unease.

'The Traveller's Prophecy. Lightfight-
ers will come,' answered Zephyr. 'A teacher and three children. One of them will be the Prince of Atlantis with eyes
green and deep as the sea. When they arrive, the battle will
commence.'

Finn gulped, closed his green eyes.

'There is great power here. Power in you, Hareb, and in
you children. Who are you?' murmured the Djinn Lord.

Shamal stepped off the carpet. He sang to his father in
that mesmerizing lilt. It had the cadences and beauty of the
muezzin call, but a plaintiveness too.

Finally, Shamal fell silent.

Finn felt Zephyr stirring around him, scrutinising
him.

'My son thinks you might be the Prince of Atlantis.
Are you?'

Finn looked away, across the endless expanse of sand,
stretching out seemingly forever below him. There seemed
to be nowhere for him to hide, in any of the worlds. He
glanced at Shamal, saw warmth and compassion in his eyes,

and something else, a hardness, a ruthlessness he hadn't noticed before.

He turned to where he felt the heart of the wind to be and he gazed at it.

'Yes,' he answered simply, defiance, regret and acceptance warring in his eyes. 'I am.'

CHAPTER TWELVE

❧ Another War ❧

ZEPHYR LET OUT A great sigh, an exhalation, it seemed to Finn, of relief. Shamal's eyes gleamed with fierce delight. He was yearning for this battle with an intensity that troubled Finn.

'Good gracious Finn!' exclaimed Hareb. 'I always thought there was something different about you. But this...' his words tailed off in wonder. He turned to Georgie and Fred.

'Always felt that about the three of you, actually. It's in your eyes, rich with secrets and awareness, and it's in the way you carry yourselves. It's like a whiff of foreignness, only it's a foreignness I've never seen before and I've travelled a lot.'

'I felt it about you, too,' replied Finn. 'That you had secrets. And power.'

'You are miraculous, the three of you,' intoned Zephyr. 'You are true LightFighters. But you walked into your destiny young, so young.' His voice was poignant. 'And now you have walked into another battle. Into another war.'

CHAPTER THIRTEEN

∽ Attack ∽

'WHAT WAR?' ASKED FINN. He got off the carpet. He feared that he was being rude but he felt a sudden and overwhelming urge to flee this place, however beautiful it was, however captivating Shamal might be, however mesmerising Zephyr was. He wanted to be lounging on his beanbag in his room at Aunt C's house, with Georgie and Fred on beanbags beside him, eating Georgie's world-class brownies.

'The war that Typhon is waging,' said Shamal, voice hard.

'The Travellers saw you and Typhon together,' Zephyr told Finn. 'The Travellers say Typhon fears you will destroy him. You were prophesied to fight him.'

'But why me?' asked Finn. 'Again, why me? Why is this my war?' He asked the question with the battle-weariness of one who had looked death in the eye too closely and too frequently.

'Maktoob. Because it is written,' said Zephyr.

'And who are these Travellers?' demanded Finn, as if all his problems could be laid at their door.

'They are humans, a very dangerous type of human. They are Seers, they can read the future. Some say that they can project their minds into the future, and that is how they See, others say that some of them, the most powerful, perhaps one every few hundred years, can ride the Winds of Time, travel back and forth and tell what they have seen.'

'What are the Winds of –' Finn began to ask. A scream of agony ripped across his words. Shamal cried out again. He fell to the ground and curled up into a ball, groaning in agony.

Zephyr gave a roar of rage. He curled himself round his son. Georgie felt the bands of wind coiling round Shamal, she could see their outlines shimmering. Shamal started to twitch and flinch as if he were having a fit. Georgie, Fred and Hareb leapt off the carpet and stood watching, paralysed. Georgie felt the rage and the pain of Zephyr as he arched around his son.

'What's happening?' she cried.

Finn shook his head, confused and horrified. Shamal had saved their lives and now it looked as if he were dying. Finn reached out, tried to touch Shamal's agonised face. His fingers stopped short. Zephyr had made a force-field around his son and Finn couldn't touch him.

'Someone's hurting him,' wailed Georgie, 'he looks like he's being attacked by something invisible.'

'And not even his father can stop it,' said Finn through gritted teeth.

'Something gets through the force-field,' said Fred. 'God, this is horrible. Stop!' he moaned. 'Whoever it is, please stop.'

Hareb looked on in powerless horror, desperate to do something, anything, but he didn't know what and he didn't know how.

Again there was the sound of distant thunder echoing around the battlements.

The agonised twitching seemed to go on for hours, though it must have been just minutes. When it looked as if Shamal's body could take no more, he gave a huge shudder and fell still.

CHAPTER FOURTEEN

The Sacred Covenant

G EORGIE GASPED IN HORROR.
'It's over. For now,' said Zephyr with a voice as heavy as lead.

Fred was shaking his head. 'He's not…he's not…?'

'No,' replied Zephyr, 'he's not dead. Not this time.'

Shamal let out a moan and his eyes flickered open. He sat up groggily, and ran a hand over his face. His skin was unnaturally pale. His eyes were tormented.

Georgie reached across to him, took his hand.

'What happened?'

Shamal rubbed his face ferociously. Slowly, his colour returned.

'I have a sister,' he rasped, struggling under the weight of a great emotion.

'A twin sister, Mistral. She is twenty.'

'Twenty!' exclaimed Georgie. 'But you said she was a twin!'

'She is. Typhon kidnapped her ten years ago, when she and I were ten. He uses her powers, and through her, he has a way into me and my powers. We should have grown older, bigger, but he takes our energy, our growth and uses it for himself. We will grow no older. We will stay forever ten.'

'Like Peter Pan,' mused Georgie.

'Yes, but unlike Peter Pan, we *do* want to grow up. Typhon has trapped our bodies in time and trapped my sister in space. He keeps her locked in a room of lead so that she cannot communicate with me. She is a Seer, and lead blocks her vision. When he wants to use her powers he takes her out, lets her see the light of the stars, and then she can See and communicate with me too. Sometimes, if I am lucky, and if she is thinking of me deeply, I can get through the lead walls and communicate with her in her prison, but normally she needs the stars. When Typhon needs her vision she is released from her cell. The other weeks, days, hours, seconds, she lives in a lead room, twelve feet by twelve feet. She sees no light. She feels no breeze. She sees no-one. Speaks to no-one. Can you imagine?' he whispered his horror. 'Can you imagine how that feels?'

Georgie shook her head sorrowfully while Fred gazed into space, eyes horrified. Finn stared at the ground, his features rigid with rage.

'How dare he?' he said, in a whisper almost to himself. He raised his eyes to Shamal. 'Why did he take her? There must be other Seers, Dark creatures like himself?'

Zephyr answered, voice staccato with fury. 'He took her because he is evil, and because he wants to use the power of my own children against me and in doing that he is killing them. And he took her as a hostage, so that I will never be able to attack him without killing my own daughter.'

'Why does he want to use your children's power against you?' asked Finn.

'He wants to defeat me. He wants to become the sole Storm Djinn and to live forever.'

'The Eternity Project, he calls it,' continued Zephyr. 'We know, through Mistral communicating with Shamal, that Typhon is collecting Talismans, objects of great power he believes will help him live forever, and which will help him defeat me. You see I have one power he doesn't. I can travel through time. He cannot. He believes that with his Talismans he can defeat me, steal my powers, then he will break the Sacred Covenant and he will hold history in his hand. He will mould it this way and that. If you control history, you control the future, so the planet, and all life on it, will be forever his. And let's not forget who he is, what he is. Typhon is Dark Matter. He kills what he is near.'

Georgie, Fred and Finn exchanged appalled glances.

'What's the Sacred Covenant?' asked Fred.

'I can travel through time,' answered Zephyr, 'but I am forbidden to change the past. That is the Code and The Covenant. If I break those, then the world and all in it could fall.'

'So you cannot go back in time and stop Zephyr stealing your daughter,' said Georgie.

'However much I yearn to,' replied Zephyr, his voice strained with anguish. 'When he is angry he punishes Mistral, and through her, Shamal too. Her pain is his pain. What she feels, he feels. That is why Typhon can get through my force-field. I cannot block him.'

'He nearly killed her this time,' croaked Shamal.

'I saw,' replied his father, all his pain and his fury condensed into those two words.

'I've never felt such rage from him,' said Shamal. 'It is because you escaped him,' he said to Hareb. He turned to Finn. 'And because you escaped him too. He was hunting you as well. He must have felt your power, made the link between you and the Prophecy. One teacher, three children, one with formidable Power. I felt your Power as soon as I saw you. He will have done too. He will stop at nothing now until he kills you.'

Finn suppressed a shudder.

'What can we do?' asked Georgie. 'What can we do to help Mistral?'

'How do we fight him?' asked Fred.

'It is my battle now,' said Finn. 'If it is prophesied, bring it on. I want to fight him, more than anything I want to fight him. And I want to kill him.'

'Are you sure?' asked Zephyr. 'You know what is at stake?'

'I've always known,' replied Finn, 'from the first battle.' He turned to Fred and Georgie, 'but not you two. Not again. You must go home and –'

'Not again!' shouted Georgie. 'Do you *never* learn. We are *all* in this. I want to fight him too.'

'I do too,' said Fred fiercely.

'Zephyr said three children would come to start the war. *Three* children not one,' continued Georgie at a yell.

There was a soft clearing of the throat. 'Er, is this a private fight or can anyone join in?' asked Hareb. 'Because I'd rather like to fight Typhon as well, if that's all right,' he said mildly. 'He killed my friend, Axel, I'm sure of that. He would have killed me. And according to the Travellers, it would seem that I have a bit of a part to play in this battle too.'

Everyone fell silent. Finn's beleaguered look began to fade, as did Georgie's look of outrage and Fred's of manic determination.

'All of us,' said Georgie.

'Or none of us,' added Fred.

'Precisely!' concurred Hareb.

'Well, then,' said Finn, 'I suppose it'd better be all of us.'

Chapter Fifteen

☙ Time to Go ☙

'So, how do we -' Hareb began to ask. He was interrupted by Shamal shouting: 'Mistral! She's communicating!'

Shamal stood, eyes closed, swaying gently.

Abruptly, his eyes flew open. He spoke urgently.

'Mistral can See you, here with me. She knows the Battle starts with you. She is recovering. She offers you her thanks and her blessings. But you *must* go. Now. Mistral can See the rescue services approaching the dunes near the burnt-out car. I'm coming with you,' announced Shamal.

'I'll live in my old house. We'll work on a plan together.'

'Stay safe in the world, child of my heart,' warned Zephyr, 'veil yourself. The world of man does not welcome those who are different, who do not fit the narrow mould.'

'I know, Father. I will take care. I promise.'

Shamal turned to the others.

'Time to go back to your world. Are you ready?'

'Ready!' They all replied in unison. Hareb's eyes shone with anticpation.

'Hold tight,' said Shamal.

They grasped hands. There was the great rushing sound, the feeling of G force sucked the breath from their lungs and then they were lying on the sand, bodies strewn like wreckage. The smoke billowed gently from the burning car. Nothing else moved.

CHAPTER SIXTEEN

❧ The Policeman ❧

MOMENTS LATER, A VEHICLE crested the dune and rolled down slowly towards them. Four men, two in kandooras, one in a policeman's uniform and one in shorts and a tee shirt jumped out, leaving the car doors open. They rushed down to the bodies.

'My God,' wailed the man in the tee shirt. 'No, they can't be. Please tell me they can't be,' he pleaded, his lilting Welsh accent tremulous with fear.

Georgie felt the thud of footsteps running towards her. She felt breath on her neck. She rolled over slowly and opened her eyes.

'Oh thank goodness!' exclaimed the same voice, almost ecstatic with relief.

'Mr Jones?' Georgie said groggily, recognising the school P.E. teacher, the man in charge of the whole trip.

'This one's alive too,' called the policeman, standing over Finn. His voice was oddly dispassionate. He was tall, powerfully-built. Combat-ready, thought Finn, sitting up, eyeing him warily.

'And this one! And this one!' called out the robed figures.

Slowly, Georgie, Fred and Hareb sat up. 'Yes, alhamdullilah,' intoned Hareb. '*We* are all indeed alive.' He paused, eyes sweeping the dunes. 'But our driver, Shaukat, is missing.' He pointed. 'He went to the top of that dune to try to get a signal for his mobile, to ring for help. He didn't come back.'

'Did you go to look for him?' asked the policeman, sharply.

Georgie frowned in surprise. The man's eyes were hard, hostile.

Hareb shook his head. 'We tried to shelter from the shamal. We could hardly move. We hunkered down here.'

'Then passed out?' queried the policeman, not attempting to hide his disbelief.

No, we entered the Kingdom of the Storm Djinn, thought Finn. *We sat on a hovering carpet in the Castle of the Winds and spoke of good and evil and war.*

The policeman wheeled round as if he had read Finn's thoughts.

'What, exactly, has been going on h–' he started to ask.

'Mwwaaah!' sobbed Georgie, loudly, theatrically and quite convincingly. 'I want my mother,' she wailed. 'I want to go home. Now.' She added a few more sobs for good measure.

The policeman stared at her, sceptically.

'My head!' yelled Fred, swaying back and forth, cradling his head in his hands. 'Ow, it hurts. It hurts so much. Eouiwww!' he yelled again.

'We must get these children out of here, back to their parents as soon as possible,' said Hareb, rising to his feet. 'They are in shock. And they are injured. Look at those bruises.'

The kandooraed Emiratis made sounds of agreement, frowning discreetly at the policeman.

'That's imperative,' announced Mr Jones firmly, his Welsh accent becoming more singsong as his worry rose. 'Get them back with the rest of the party, then start back for Dubai.'

'Just one second,' said the policeman slowly, drawing a pad from his pocket with the same deliberate menace as if it were a revolver. He turned back to Finn. Wordlessly, he studied him. Finn tried to make himself as grey and uninteresting as possible.

'I would like to take down your names, ages, phone numbers and P.O. Box numbers. If you don't mind,' he declared, as if daring anybody to mind.

Finn cast quick glances at Georgie and Fred. Their own eyes mirrored his disquiet.

They gave their names and phone numbers, each independently transposing a few numbers.

'School?' asked the policeman. 'Who is responsible for this…*trip*,' he finished, rolling the word around his mouth as if in distaste.

'Jumeirah Academy of Music,' answered Hareb. 'May I ask,' he began cordially, 'why we are being questioned?'

The policeman eyed him narrowly.

'We found your driver, Shaukat, wand –'

'Oh thank Goodness!' exclaimed Georgie. 'That's fantastic! He's ali–'

'As I was saying,' cut in the policeman, 'we found your driver in a state of distress. He said that he came back down the dune to look for you. He said that you had all gone. He said that you had *disappeared*.'

'Disappeared?' intoned Hareb, as if he had just heard something most amusing. 'As in, popped down to Starbucks for a cappuccino to wait out the shamal?'

Finn, Fred and Georgie burst out laughing. The policeman shot them a look that made the laughter freeze on their lips.

'The visibility was practically zero,' said Hareb, his voice serious now. 'The only way we stayed together was by holding hands. Of course he couldn't see us. The shamal hid us.'

That much was true, thought Georgie. Shamal *did* hide us.

The policeman studied Hareb for a moment. 'Is that right?' he asked slowly.

Finn's alarm bells started to clang hysterically in his head. He knew that measuring look. This was no ordinary policeman. This man was a Seer and Finn absolutely, categorically, one hundred per cent did *not* want him to see into Hareb's head. So he staged a faint, collapsing dramatically onto the sand. He lay there, eyes closed, concentrating on blankness, filling his mind with the image of a wall of sand. He felt the policeman's eyes turn to him, felt the man's mind probing his own, felt the flash of frustration and rage when the policeman met the wall of sand and got no further. But the policeman didn't give up. He probed deeper. Finn's brain felt as if it were burning, but he forced himself to lie still, face impassive, as the pain roiled around his head.

'Finn! Finn boyo. Wake up!' urged Mr Jones, crouching down beside Finn, worriedly feeling for a pulse. He found one, then stared angrily at the policeman.

'I must insist that we get these children home, or to a hospital.'

The policeman turned away from Finn and gave Mr Jones a hard look. Finn exhaled in relief as the scrutiny and the pain ceased. He gave it half a minute then opened his eyes groggily.

'Er, what?' he mumbled, sitting up slowly.

'Phew!' exclaimed Mr Jones. 'Had me worried there Finn. Now, let's get you up and back to - '

'Just one question, then you may go,' cut in the police-man. He turned to Hareb. 'You haven't explained to me why you were all lying on the sand when we found you, apparently unconscious.'

He flicked a glance at Finn, Fred and Georgie. 'Did he hurt you, this man, in any way?'

Hareb's face creased with fury, but he said nothing.

'Of course he didn't,' exclaimed Fred, outraged.

'No way!' shouted Georgie.

'No. He absolutely did not,' replied Finn icily.

'Satisfied?' asked Hareb, voice clipped with suppressed fury.

'No. Not really. But for now, go. You're free,' he said in almost contemptuous dismissal. But then he turned back towards them.

'I know where to find you,' he added. 'If I need you.'

Chapter Seventeen

⊂⊃ Home ⊂⊃

'WHAT? BACK ALREADY?' EXCLAIMED Aunt C, squinting into the sunlight as Georgie and Finn walked through the door.

'Your cheek!' she shrieked when she saw Georgie's face. 'And Finn, you look rough. What on earth happened?'

'Let them get in the house first, Camelia,' said Georgie's father. He took their camping bags and led them into the kitchen. Georgie's younger sisters, the twins Cressida and Cordelia, crowded round noisily demanding to know why she and Finn were back.

'Give them a minute,' cautioned their father.

He put on the kettle and brewed up a pot of tea. Only when he had handed out four cups, adding generous lashings of milk and sugar did he sit down expectantly.

Georgie and Finn nursed their cups, sipping the sweet, hot liquid with relief, eyes flickering around the sitting room, both thinking the same thoughts. *Home*, so good to be home, but thinking too of Mistral, so far from her home.

'There was a shamal,' said Georgie. 'Our car turned over.' Aided by Finn, she told her parents and sisters a severely edited version of the truth.

'Well, no-one was hurt, thank goodness,' concluded her father. 'And we'll go to the Empty Quarter another time. Make up for it, hey?'

Georgie and Finn nodded. Aunt C, scrutinising them closely, put down their lack of enthusiasm to exhaustion.

'Early to bed for you two, I'd say.'

When Finn and Georgie nodded their agreement without a hint of a fight, her suspicions multiplied like a virus.

'Johnny, something happened out there in the Empty Quarter,' she said to her husband when all the children were asleep that night.

'Yes,' he replied with quiet patience. 'They had a nasty roll in a car.'

Camelia shook her head. 'No. It was more than that.'

'Isn't that enough to shake them up a bit?'

'It takes more than that after all they have been through.'

'Perhaps,' mused Johnny, recalling the faraway looks in Georgie and Finn's eyes.

'I am going to keep a close eye on them,' declared Camelia. 'Something's up. I can practically smell it.'

Chapter Eighteen

Fred's Inquisition

I N HIS HOUSE OVERLOOKING the sea, Fred was subjected to an inquisition by his mother and a rant from his father.

'Poor Freddie. Are you really all right?' crooned his mother, holding an ice pack to Fred's bruised forehead. At the same time, his father muttered threats.

'Outrageous, rolling a car. Could have been killed. Think I'll talk to my lawyer. Negligence, pure negligence.'

'No,' pleaded Fred. 'It wasn't the driver's fault. There was a shamal, a terrible shamal. Anyone could have rolled a car, even you.'

'I am an investment banker. Your idiot driver, is a driver. It's his job *not* to roll cars.'

'So sue the shamal,' snapped Fred with uncharacteristic spleen. His father's belief that there was no problem that could not be solved with money and a lawyer drove Fred mad. He knew his father just wanted to fix things, but didn't he know there were some things that just couldn't be fixed, not even with the magic of money?

Fred's father gaped at him open-mouthed like a fish.

'He's tired. In shock still,' said his mother quickly, shooting her husband a look. 'Let's get him to bed then we can discuss what to do.'

'Please,' said Fred, getting up and gently removing his mother's hand from his forehead. 'There *is* nothing to do. I just want to sleep then go back to school as normal. I don't want anyone to be sued. I don't want you to hassle the school, Dad, or Adventure Rangers. Please,' he repeated.

His father glared into the distance, then turned back to Fred and studied him for a moment. An unusual softness stole into his eyes. 'O.K. Freddie. If that's what you really want,' he said quietly.

Fred exhaled with relief. For his father to back down was most unusual.

Fred gave him a big hug. 'Thanks, Dad. It *is* what I want.'

His mother hugged them both. *Home*, Fred thought with relief. *Make the most of it, while you can,* said the voice of the LightFighter in his brain.

Chapter Nineteen

❧ New Boy ❧

INN, FRED AND GEORGIE'S class was unusually subdued the next day. They sat at their desks, pulling out their books, collecting dictionaries, thesauruses, sharpened pencils, rubbers – all they would need for the creative writing assignment that had been set for them. It was meant to be a story about the Empty Quarter. Fred groaned inwardly. The truth would have made the best story ever. He was going to have to be very creative and aim for dullness. He decided he was going to write a story about a desert rat.

He glanced around the classroom, searching for inspiration. Instead he noted the cupped hands, the heads angled together so that no-one could overhear, the covert glances flicked towards him, Finn and Georgie. He wondered what they were saying, the whisperers.

The whispering stopped as Hareb stalked into the classroom. Finn felt his presence before he saw him. Hareb seemed to carry around his own personal force-field, call it magnetism, call it charisma, or else just a fierce intellect matched by an unyielding will. It made it easy for him to manage his class. There was a look in his eyes which dissuaded all but the most rebellious, or unseeing, from challenging him.

Finn glanced up at him and gasped. Standing just behind Hareb, gazing out at the sea of faces with a look of open curiosity, was Shamal.

'Good morning class,' intoned Hareb. 'We have a new student joining us. Please say hello to Shaheel Sultan. And make him at home, would you?'

Finn, Fred and Georgie found their voices.

'Hello Shaheel,' they chorused, along with the rest of the class.

Hareb guided Shaheel to a spare seat at a table beside Hugh Cleverly, Tom Wilder and Lara Lions. A good table, thought Finn. They were not whisperers, those three. Unlike the table behind him. There, the motley group of Brian Dundas, whom they called Bovine because of his habit of chewing gum in a cow-like manner, Nicole Jones who was a vicious gossip and Colin Weeks whom they called Butthead for reasons anyone who set eyes on his face could appreciate, sat muttering while they scrutinised the newcomer with all the friendliness of cannibals on feast day. Vlad Czarovich, who had the misfortune to share their table, bestowed a lugubrious smile upon the newcomer and turned conspicuously away from the trio of whisperers.

Break seemed an age in coming. Finn burned with impatience. Finally the bell sounded. Shamal got to his feet and removed something from his backpack that looked like a baton. He thudded it against the palm of his hand, eyes thoughtful as he headed into the corridor. Fred contrived to fall into line next to him.

'Hi,' he said jovially. 'My name's Fred. Like to come and share our acacia tree?'

Shamal raised his eyebrows a fraction. 'Doesn't your mother give you a snack?'

'Ha ha, very funny,' chimed Georgie, coming along-side. 'It's just where we hang out, me, Fred and Finn.' Georgie pointed, acting out her charade for the benefit of all the onlookers studying them with interest. 'He's the one that looks like a surf dude with the long hair and the green eyes over there.'

Finn weakly raised a hand, as if half-heartedly greeting a stranger.

Shamal nodded, an amused smile playing across his lips. 'What happens if anybody else sits there?'

'They don't.'

'Why? You beat them up or something?'

'Do I look the type?' quizzed Georgie.

'No,' replied Shamal, shaking his head. He'd already noticed their separateness, how Finn, Fred and Georgie, now all walking beside him, seemed to have their own little force-field around them, keeping everyone at a distance.

CHAPTER TWENTY

∽ The Ankh ∽

THE ACACIA TREE WAS, of course, unoccupied. They sat down cross-legged in its shade, Finn, Fred and Georgie collapsing their limbs into position, while Shamal sank to the ground with elegant economy. Even in the JAM uniform of green and black striped shorts, short-sleeved white shirt and blue tie he looked exotic, like a young Bedouin prince.

When they were sure there was no-one within earshot, Georgie spoke.

'Right. Spill Shamal, or Shaheel, rather. What the heck are you doing here?'

'What, not pleased to see me?'

'Very pleased,' answered Finn.

'Just surprised,' added Fred.

'We need to plot and plan,' said Shamal. 'What better place to do it than at your school.'

And, thought Finn, what better place to keep an eye on the three of them, to remind them about Mistral and Typhon and the other world which might have been easy for some to forget.

'I know you haven't forgotten about my sister, or Typhon or the battle,' said Shamal, as if he had read Finn's mind. 'But time is short. Something happened last night after you had gone.'

Shamal tapped the baton against his hand, then unfurled it.

'Today's Times newspaper?' queried Fred, perplexed. '*Extremists in rampage,*' he intoned, reading the headline. '*Betrayed on Yacht, claims M.P*, er, what does this have to do with us?' he asked.

'See this little headline,' replied Shamal, pointing.

Finn twisted round to read it: '*Tornado hits M4. Multiple pile up. Two killed. Tutankhamen's Ankh stolen.*' He raised a questioning eyebrow at Shamal.

'Typhon?'

Shamal nodded.

Finn read on. *'A tornado hit the westbound side of the M4 motorway yesterday evening at the height of rush-hour, killing two. The wind blew in from nowhere, claimed witnesses. 'One minute it was calm, then next this wind hit us like a tank,' claimed Mr Brian Cox from Huddersfield who was on his way to Heathrow to catch a flight to Halifax, Nova Scotia. 'Blew me right over. Luckily the traffic was slow-moving.'*

The Met Office failed to predict the tornado, but a spokesperson, when questioned claimed that 'there was no weather paradigm for this. There were none of the warning signs. This was a completely freak phenomenon,' she added. The two dead were the driver and the security guard in a heavily armed Securicor truck which was believed to be carrying artefacts from the Tutankhamen exhibition from the O2 arena to Heathrow airport where they were due to be flown back to the National Museum of Cairo. See page seven for details.'

Finn flicked to page 7. Georgie took the paper and read, her elfin features almost vixen-like in concentration.

'The organisers of the Tutankhamen exhibition which has just closed in O2 confirmed last night that the Securicor van which was lifted into the air and blown fifty feet into a field beside the M4 was carrying priceless artefacts from the exhibition. 'Tutankhamen's Ankh has disappeared,' they confirmed. 'There is now an international search underway for the Ankh, which was the ancient Egyptian's symbol of eternal life. The Ankh is two feet high and is made of 22 carat gold.' A spokeswoman for Sotheby's Europe said last night that it was impossible to put a price on the Ankh. 'An artefact of that nature is beyond price,' she commented. The Metropolitan Police declined to comment but witnesses claim they saw a man appear just after the truck crashed down into the field. They saw the same man running from the scene, carrying what looked like a heavy steel box. Witnesses further claimed that the man then disappeared into a wooded area. The National Museum of Cairo's Director, Muhammad Ismail, says he is 'devastated by the theft of the Ankh and appeals to the thief to hand it back for the sake of history.'

'So Typhon caused a tornado?' asked Georgie, laying down the newspaper and looking up at Shamal. 'Metamorphosised and stole the Ankh?' she continued.

'Another Talisman for the Eternity Project,' suggested Finn.

'Exactly,' replied Shamal.

'How many Talismans does he have?' asked Fred.

'Five,' replied Shamal. 'Mistral has told me that he seeks two more. The Book of the Dead, which is rumoured to be in the National Museum in Cairo, and Tutankhamen's Burial Shroud, woven in the finest gold mesh, which was reputedly stolen from the tombs as Lord Carnarvon was excavating them. It's never been seen since. It might not even exist.'

'How did he know,' mused Georgie, 'that the Ankh would be on the way to Heathrow at exactly that time and in exactly that vehicle?'

'Mistral,' replied Shamal simply. 'Typhon asked her to track it. He knew the exhibition had closed and that the artefacts would soon be on the move. Mistral cannot locate stationary objects, but, if they move, she can. She tracked it to the M4 near London. She communicated with me last night, warned me that Typhon was on the trail of the Ankh. It will now be in his Dark Kingdom, with the other Talismans.'

'And, if whoever holds the Book of the Dead and the Burial Shroud, if it exists, starts to feel nervous because of the theft of the Ankh, and decides to move them,' said Finn thinking quickly, 'then Mistral can track them and Typhon can blow in and grab them.'

'Precisely.'

'Can she lie, Mistral?' asked Fred.

Shamal shook his head. 'She cannot lie about her visions. She is a Seer of the Light, a soothsayer, a truthteller.'

'So the clock is ticking,' said Finn. 'When Typhon gets the other Talismans he will attack your father.'

'Yes. He will,' confirmed Shamal.

'Will the Talismans really give him eternal life?' asked Fred.

'We don't know,' replied Shamal. 'Typhon is thousands of years old. You acquire a lot of knowledge in a life that long. So, who knows, perhaps they will work, perhaps they won't, but Typhon believes they will.'

Finn nodded. 'And belief is the most powerful weapon of all,' he said, recalling Mr. Violet, the extraordinary teacher who had materialised at JAM, taught them lessons more valuable than jewels, before he became a victim of the Dark Sea Djinn.

Shamal glanced appraisingly at Finn. 'You know a lot, for one so young. And you are right. Belief is a shield of armour, the heaviest sword. If Typhon beats my father, if he kills him, then there will be nothing and no-one standing between him and earth. He will blow through again, destroy all that stands, eradicate all that lives.'

'An extinction event,' said Fred, eyes wide with horror. 'Like the dinosaurs, obliterated from the face of the earth.'

CHAPTER TWENTY ONE

↝ The Plan ↜

'SO HOW DO WE stop Typhon getting his hands on the other Talismans?' asked Georgie.

Finn smiled and his eyes glittered as he voiced his plan.

'We get there first. We steal the Talismans ourselves.'

'We what?' exclaimed Georgie.

Shamal rocked back on his heels, chuckling.

'I like you, Prince of Atlantis,' he said, 'you have vision.'

'And then,' continued Finn, 'we use the artefacts as bait. We suggest a trade to Typhon; a Talisman in exchange for Mistral.'

'Brilliant!' cried Shamal. 'He will try to double cross you of course.'

Finn smiled, 'And so will we try to double cross him. We will try to trap him. Somewhere he won't be able to escape from, won't be able to harm us, or anyone. Question is how and where. *That* we need to work out.'

Shamal grinned so much his teeth flashed white. He made Georgie think of a shark, in sight of its prey.

'Fabulous idea,' said Fred, 'can't fault the logic. But how, exactly, are we going to steal two heavily guarded Talismans, one of which might not even exist, let alone –'

The bell rang drowning out the rest of Fred's question. Reluctantly the four students left the shade of the acacia tree and walked into the dazzling sunlight. The call of the muezzin drifted through the shimmering air, distorted but strong.

Belief, thought Finn. 'We'll find a way,' he said.

The next lesson was numeracy, but neither Finn, Georgie, Fred nor Shamal was able to concentrate. They all gazed out of the window, eyes superficially taking in the towering vision of Burj Dubai, but seeing in their minds' eyes the Castle of the Winds, a battle, an Ankh, the Book of the Dead and a Burial Shroud that may not even exist.

After giving them three warnings, Hareb snapped.

'Right. No more warnings. Detention for Finn, Fred, Georgie and Shama-er Shaheel, first day or not. I'll just go and ring your parents, tell them to come and get you an hour later than normal.'

Butthead conspicuously failed to get detention despite Hareb catching him throwing an eraser at Vlad's head from across the classroom. The class watched him open-mouthed as he said merely, distractedly: 'Good shot. Perhaps you should take up golf with hand-eye coordination like that!'

Vlad glowered and muttered darkly in Russian. Georgie watched him worriedly, resolving to warn Hareb to tread lightly with Vlad. Neither Hareb, nor any of the rest of the class knew that Vlad's father had been Jehannem, the Dark Fire Djinn. Half Djinn, Vlad had undreamt of powers. The fact that he didn't seem to know that, or use them, didn't make him any less scary. Butthead too was almost literally playing with fire.

CHAPTER TWENTY TWO

∽ Astral Travel ∽

'AT LAST,' SAID HAREB when the final bell rang and the rest of the class had filed out. He closed the door and perched on the edge of his desk.

'You four are miles away. In another kingdom, I'd say.' He leaned forward, eyes sharp. 'What's going on?'

Shamal showed him the newspaper, the two articles. Hareb's eyes widened in amazement.

'So Typhon blew across to London, caused a tornado, materialised as a man and ran off with the Ankh?'

'He can manifest as anything he wants,' said Shamal.

'Jehannem, the Dark Fire Djinn spent a lot of time as a man,' explained Georgie. 'He built up businesses, lived as a man for much of the time.'

'So there could be other Djinn, living amongst us, unknown?' asked Hareb.

'The most powerful ones, yes,' replied Shamal. 'And creatures like me. I am half djinn after all.'

Georgie grinned. 'And I don't think anyone in the class has a clue.'

Fred shook his head. 'I saw Vlad looking at you, Shamal. Watching you.'

'Who is Vlad?' asked Shamal.

'The skinhead on your table,' replied Finn.

'You need to know this too, Hareb,' said Georgie. 'Vlad's half Djinn. Jehannem's his father.'

Shamal jumped up. 'He's half Dark Djinn?'

'He is, but don't worry. He's healed. He's on our side now, and his father's dead,' said Georgie, praying that were true.

'Are you sure?' asked Shamal, unease flickering in his amber eyes.

'As sure as we can be,' answered Finn. 'We need to talk about the plan,' he continued, keen to move on. Quickly, he told Hareb.

Hareb smiled.

'So, step one is to find the Book of the Dead,' Hareb declared. He got up and walked across to his computer. 'Let's Google it.'

'Book of the Dead,' he read, 'believed to have been the personal copy of Tutankhamen, the book is purported to reveal the steps necessary to move from life on earth to eternal life in the Netherworld. Rumoured to be kept in secret vaults in the National Museum in Cairo, but exact whereabouts unknown.'

'That's helpful,' said Georgie sarcastically. 'Given that we need to steal it, they might at least have the decency to tell us where it is.'

'Maybe we could frighten them into moving it,' suggested Fred. 'Then Mistral could track it.'

'Then both Typhon and we will be trying to steal it,' pointed out Georgie.

'Then we'll just have to get there first,' said Finn.

'How on earth will we do that?' asked Hareb. 'Chartering a private jet is a bit out of my league.'

Finn smiled. 'We don't need a private jet.'

'What do you mean?' asked Hareb.

'It's not just Shamal who can Astral Travel, or make others travel with him,' answered Finn. 'We can Astral Travel too.'

'Can you really?' asked Hareb.

'Watch,' replied Finn with a grin. He visualised the flat roof of the school. He remembered Mr. Violet's words of advice on how to Astral Travel. He *Saw*. He *Believed*. He *Leapt*.

CHAPTER TWENTY THREE

An Unwelcome Visit

FINN LANDED TWENTY FEET from the edge of the flat roof on all fours like a cat. He glanced round quickly to make sure no-one had seen him, that no random maintenance was being carried out on the roof. All clear. He breathed a sigh of relief. But something nagged at him. He leopard-crawled his way to the edge of the building. He watched a car approaching the school at speed. It ignored the parking spaces outside and swung in through the main entrance. A door was flung open even before it came to a halt and out stepped a powerfully built man. Finn gasped. It was the policeman from the Empty Quarter.

Another man got out beside him, tall and thin with a hard, elongated face. They studied the school building. Finn stared down at them, heart pumping. He could hear sounds from the road, parents muttering into their mobiles as they arrived late to pick up their children. He strained to hear the two men's conversation. His powers had developed over the past year, his eye sight and hearing were sharp as a hunting animal. He turned his head, tuning in.

'All here…three of them….who exactly…they are….is the Prince…Atlantis or not.'

Suddenly the policeman glanced up, as if aware that he was being watched. Finn flattened himself against the roof and listened. There was silence for a moment, then the policeman's voice drifted up to Finn.

'Someone's watching….ightFi….I *know* it.'

Finn waited a few beats, then raised his head just in time to see both men striding into the building.

Finn crawled back from the edge. He took a moment, composed himself, focused. Seconds later, he re-materialised in Hareb's classroom.

'Finn!' exclaimed Hareb. 'So you ca - '

'The policeman's coming,' Finn interrupted. 'The one from the Empty Quarter. And I've a feeling he's coming for us. We need to get out of here. Now.'

CHAPTER TWENTY FOUR

The
Black Hummer

HAREB GRABBED HIS BRIEFCASE and pulled out a set of car keys.

'Black Hummer. Can't miss it. Get in it and hide. Go, now. All of you.'

'What're you going to do?' asked Finn, moving towards the door.

'Diversionary tactics. Now *go!*'

Finn, Fred, Georgie and Shamal rushed from the classroom and ran down the corridor. Just after they turned the corner, they heard Hareb's voice.

They didn't pause, just raced along the next corridor, down the back stairs and out to the teachers' car park. The black Hummer was easy to spot. Finn clicked on the keys and the lights flashed in welcome. They hurried over, let themselves into the back and hunkered down on the floor. Finn clicked the doors locked. The windows were tinted. No-one could see in. They were safe. For now.

Hareb nudged his sunglasses and adjusted his shemargh in a gesture of impatience.

'I repeat. Can I help you?' he said in his most supercilious voice. Standing tall in his kandoora, he made an impressive figure. He felt the policeman's eyes boring into him. He returned the glare.

'Do you have a pass, from Reception?' Hareb added, with an officious smile.

'We don't need a pass,' grunted the policeman, taking a step closer.

Hareb stood his ground and smiled. He knew a bully when he saw one. He hated them whatever age they were.

'Oh, but there you are wrong, my friend. Everybody needs a pass. After all, you could be impostors, could you not?' He took his mobile from his pocket and hit a number.

'Yes, security. Mr Al Suwaidi here. Please come to my classroom. Two gentlemen,' he emphasised the word in faint ridicule, 'need a couple of passes.'

He clicked off. 'Names?' he asked.

'Colonel Raheem,' answered the policeman.

Hareb turned to see the other man stepping behind him to open the door to the classroom.

'Excuse me,' Hareb said sternly. 'I really must insist.'

'Not here,' said the other man after peering in.

'Who is not here?' asked Hareb.

'Let's go,' said the Policeman. 'We're wasting time.'

The two men headed away just as the security guards came hurrying up the stairs. They looked questioningly at Hareb.

'Watch them,' said the teacher. 'Make sure they leave the premises directly.'

He picked up his briefcase and hastened after them.

He took the back stairs at a run, rushed round the school to the car park and hurried up to his Hummer. Finn saw him coming and clicked open the lock. Hareb jumped in. Finn passed him the keys. Hareb started up the engine and pulled out quickly, slotting in just behind a black Mercedes.

'That them?' he asked Finn.

Finn nodded. 'What're we going to do?' he asked.

'Tail them, of course. Quick, get your seat belts on.'

The Mercedes sped off down towards Al Wasl Road. It cut into the traffic, forcing a row of cars to slam on their brakes. Hareb stayed several cars behind, keeping watch from the other lane.

'They're in a hurry, wherever they're going,' he observed, watching the Mercedes switch lanes, tailgating and bullying other cars out of its way. Hareb was forced to do the same.

'Luckily for us, people see a Hummer crowding their rearview mirror and quickly get the heck out of the way. But I never normally drive like this,' he explained.

'Needs must,' replied Georgie, bracing herself as they swung off Al Wasl onto Umm Al Sheif. The Mercedes turned onto Beach Road and roared along, ignoring the speed cameras. Hareb raced after it, cursing.

'This is going to be a very expensive ride,' he said. 'That's three speed cameras I've just sped past.'

The Mercedes swung onto the Palm Jumeirah slip road. Hareb followed and watched it turn onto one of the fronds. He quickly drove to the next frond and parked up.

'Right. Ready for a quick peek?'

The Mercedes was parked outside a large, showcase villa. Two stone lions stood guard like sentinels at either side of the front door. Luxurious foliage sprouted in the large garden. Finn caught the heady scent of jasmine, mixed with the salt tang of the sea.

'Villa 12,' said Fred

'Right,' said Hareb. 'Villa 12. I'll find out who lives

there, who Mr Policeman and his skinny friend are visiting.' He glanced at his watch. 'Quick, let's get back. Your mothers will be at school in fifteen minutes.'

CHAPTER TWENTY FIVE

∽ Coma ∽

THEY MADE IT JUST in time, turning the corner into the reception area just as Fred's mother barrelled in through the double doors.

'Frederick! Detention! Really. What have you been up to this time?' she demanded, hands on hips, chin jutted, warrior-like. She shot probing glances at Georgie, Finn and Shamal, as if she might glean the answer from them.

Fred mumbled something about concentration.

'Georgie! Finn!' announced a jovial voice - Georgie's father. He loped up, kissed Georgie on the cheek and patted Finn and Fred on the back. He turned to Fred's mother.

'Hello, Alison, how *are* you?' he asked with a beaming smile.

'Oh, er, well I'm fine actually,' she answered.

'Jolly good. Looking well. Fetching outfit.'

Fred's mother blushed. 'Thank you, Johnny.'

'Well, shall we go home then?' Johnny asked Georgie and Finn. 'Perhaps Fred would like to join us? Camelia's got something particularly delicious-smelling in the oven.'

Fred looked yearningly into his mother's eyes. He could see the battle between *Operation Perfect Son* and *Let Fred Have a Life* warring in his mother's eyes.

'Please Mum,' he prompted, leaning up to give her a kiss on the cheek.

His mother's eyes softened. *Operation Perfect Son* had largely been put on the back burner since Fred's running away to sea episode.

'O.K. then,' she said resignedly. 'I don't know why I'm being so soft.' She turned to Johnny. 'I'll pick him up at seven if that's all right?'

'Absolutely fine. Perfect.'

'I'll tell your father you had a maths Masterclass,' whispered Fred's mother.

Fred grinned. 'Thanks Mum.'

She grinned back, like the girl she once was, and then sashayed away on her high heels, turning heads, leaving in her wake a force field of perfume, like the woman she now was.

'So, you have a new partner in crime,' mused Johnny, hands slouched in his pockets, studying Shamal.

Shamal grinned. 'I'm Shaheel,' he said, stretching out his hand. Johnny shook it with a smile.

'Like to come home with us for tea too?' Johnny glanced around. 'Where's your mother, or is your father coming to get you?'

For the first time ever, Finn noticed that Shamal looked flustered.

'I'm, er, given a pretty free rein,' replied Shamal. 'I was going to walk home. I only live on Beach Road,' he explained as Johnny's eyes widened. 'But I'd love to come home with you, if I may.'

'We'd love to have you,' replied Johnny. 'But, ring your mother now, if you would, and let her know where you'll be, when to pick you up.'

Again Shamal looked perplexed.

'Here. Use my phone,' said Fred.

Shamal took the phone, tapped in some numbers, held a quick conversation and hung up.

'It's fine,' said Shamal.

Johnny nodded thoughtfully. 'O.K. Off we go.'

They sat on the beanbags in Finn's room, hands wrapped round mugs of tea, dunking Georgie's shortbread biscuits.

'Shamal, where *is* your mother?' asked Georgie.

Shamal looked away. He blew out a long sigh and turned his eyes back to Georgie.

'Here. In Dubai. At the American Hospital. Where she has been for ten years.'

'Ten years!' exclaimed Georgie.

'She's in a coma,' said Shamal with the impassivity of someone containing great emotion.

'The day Typhon took Mistral, my mother tried to protect her, to hold onto her. One minute she was standing, grabbing hold of Mistral. The next, Mistral was gone and my mother was lying on the floor. Comatose.' Shamal paused, sucked in a long, shuddering breath. 'No-one knows why she is in a coma. It's beyond medical science. They say it's possible that she could wake up anytime. But she never has.'

'Not while Typhon holds Mistral,' whispered Georgie as understanding bloomed.

'That's what I think,' agreed Shamal.

'Another reason to get Mistral back,' said Finn.

Shamal nodded.

'So, where are you living?' asked Fred.

'In my old house, on Beach Road.'

'Who's looking after you?' asked Georgie.

'I am,' answered Shamal. 'I don't need much. I can wash my own uniform, cook my own food. And if I get bored doing that, there's many more where these came from,' he said, gesturing to his clothes.

'Meaning?' asked Finn.

'Zaks, in Beach Centre.'

'You have enough money?' asked Fred.

'Who needs money, when you can Astral Travel,' replied Shamal. 'Besides, shopping when the shops are shut is so much more convenient. No queues!'

They all laughed together.

Shamal got to his feet. 'Now, talking of Astral Travel, I must go. I want to visit my mother, then return to my father for the night.'

'What'll I tell my father?' asked Georgie.

'Tell him I had to fly,' answered Shamal.

Chapter Twenty Six

⊙ Maverick ⊙

'HE'S AMAZING,' SAID GEORGIE in the silence that rang in the room after Shamal had disappeared.

'He's a maverick,' replied Finn.

'You don't trust him?' asked Fred.

Finn thought for a while. 'He wants to free his sister, free his mother from her coma. I think he'll do anything to achieve that.'

'But we want to free them too,' said Fred.

'We do,' agreed Finn. 'But we want to stay alive in the process. I think he would happily give up his own life to free his sister and mother. And ours too. What we need to do,' concluded Finn, 'is to find a way to free them, to overcome Typhon, and to stay alive.'

'I like that bit,' said Fred.

'Ditto,' agreed Georgie.

'Find the Burial Shroud,' murmured Fred.

'Find the Book of the Dead,' added Georgie.

'Fancy a trip?' asked Finn. 'Never been to Egypt.'

'We need to find out what it looks like first,' said Fred. 'It'll be in ancient Egyptian hieroglyphics, I assume,' he added.

'Don't happen to read hieroglyphics, do you Fred?' asked Finn.

'Give me a few days,' replied Fred with a grin. 'Let's get on your computer, see what we can find.'

They surfed the internet. Fred found and downloaded a Dictionary of Hieroglyphics. He stapled it together and shoved it in a huge envelope. Then they explained away Shamal's absence to a vaguely suspicious-looking Johnny.

'We need to go and see Triton,' said Fred when the three of them were ensconced back in Finn's room.

'Tricky tonight,' replied Georgie. 'My father already smells a rat. He would definitely not let us out.'

'Let's try tomorrow night then,' suggested Fred. 'We'll all try to persuade the parentals to let us go to the beach for a walk, say from five thirty to sevenish. It's pitch dark by six, so we'll have half an hour to see Triton, hopefully, and we'll be back before it's too late.'

'Sounds good,' replied Finn.

'I'll get working on it tomorrow morning,' replied Georgie. 'I'll make pancakes for breakfast. Always puts Dad in a good mood.'

'Dinneeer!' trilled Aunt C, from the bottom of the stairs.

'Great timing,' replied Georgie. 'I'm starving!'

Chapter Twenty Seven

❧ Into the Night ☙

T HEY ATE THE MOST delicious lamb with rice and chick peas and caramelised red onion, two portions each, followed by a huge family bar of milk chocolate shared between the three of them and Cordelia and Cressida, then Fred's mother whisked him home.

For the next two hours, Fred pored over the printouts from Finn's computer.

At nine forty-five, Finn said goodnight to Aunt C and Uncle Johnny and walked upstairs to his bedroom, yawning extravagantly. He took his towel from his bathroom, a bundle of clothes from his cupboard and padded them under his covers in the shape of his body. It was a ruse that had worked before and he needed it to work again now.

He listened at his door. The innocent sounds of a sleepy house, the low murmur of the television, the click of the kettle being turned on, the sharp rattle of a cup nestling into a saucer made him smile wistfully. Softly, he closed his door. He opened his window, slunk down the acacia tree, skirted across the garden and climbed over the garden wall, to freedom.

He was becoming like a cat, he thought, with this wanderlust, this yearning to get away, alone at night. He could smell the tang of the sea wafting in on the onshore breeze. Cars roared past him as he crossed Beach Road. He could hear the waves crashing on the beach now and he broke into a jog.

He turned a corner and saw before him the blank emptiness of the ocean, a dark void in the night. Only the waves were visible, foaming as they broke, catching the yellow glare of the street lamps.

Finn looked towards the Palm. He could see its lights shining like beacons across the sea guiding him.

He Saw the house with the topiary lions. He Saw the extravagant bushes, branches bowing under the weight of flowers. He smelled the rich, intoxicating waft of jasmine flowering in the night air. Then he was gone.

CHAPTER TWENTY EIGHT

∽ The Captive ∽

TWO MILES AWAY, ON the Palm, Finn landed with a rustle in a bush, breaking the central stems. He crouched in silence, gently pulling branches across him in case anyone should come out to investigate.

No-one did. He let three minutes pass, then five. He took regular peeks over the branches, but there was nothing or no-one to see at the front of the house. He extracted himself as quietly as he could from the prickly embrace of the bush and darted across the lawn to the back of the house. The curtains in all the windows were pulled shut. Odd, thought Finn, when the only people who could possibly see anything were on the opposite frond about a third of a mile away. Unless they had a telescope trained on the windows they would see nothing.

Finn gazed at the curtained glass, frustrated. He dropped to all fours and leopard-crawled across the grass to the other side of the house. There was the smallest gap in the curtains in one huge window. The light spilled out like a golden triangle on the dark of the grass.

Finn edged up to the window and peeked in.

He saw the Policeman, the skinny man with the long nose they'd seen earlier and two more men he had not seen before. They were all kicking a man who lay on the floor, hands bound behind his back. Finn felt sick. The man tried to roll away from the kicks. Finn caught a glimpse of the face, bruised, bloody, almost unrecognisable. Shaukat!

Finn stifled a gasp. He moved away from the window and stood with his back to the wall. His body throbbed with shock and rage. He wanted to shout, scream, rush into the house….. *and then what*, his voice of reason asked. He blew out a breath, breathed in and out slowly, trying to calm his mind. *Think*! He needed to rescue Shaukat, but *how?* He inched back to the crack in the curtain, just in time to see Shaukat being dragged up the stairs. Finn backed into the shadows, squeezed into a bush.

A light came on in an upstairs room, flooding the garden with a yellow pall. Finn gazed up. There was a balcony outside the room, stretching out beyond the window for about two feet on either side. He waited ten minutes. He heard nothing. Saw nothing. *This is as safe as it's going to get,* he told himself. Heart pounding, he crept back across the grass.

He jumped up, pulled himself over the railings and onto the balcony. He dropped down to the floor to the side of the window. Cautiously, he edged his head round. He saw Shaukat lying prone on a bed, arms still pinned behind his back. His ankles were also bound. Finn tried the window handle tentatively. Locked!

Inside the room, Shaukat rolled to one side, looked towards the window. His eyes opened wide when he saw Finn.

'I'll come back and get you,' mouthed Finn, exaggerating each syllable. Shaukat nodded. His eyes were desperate.

'Hurry!' he mouthed back.

Finn nodded. He focused on his bedroom, on his beanbag and jumped.

CHAPTER TWENTY NINE

Down the Acacia Tree

FINN LANDED WITH A thud. He froze, heart pounding, but there were no approaching, curious footsteps tracking down the hall or up the stairs. He padded over to his door, inched it open. The house was quiet. Aunt C and Uncle Johnny must have gone to bed. First bit of good news all evening.

He grabbed his Swiss army knife, shoved it into his pocket and tiptoed down the corridor to Georgie's room. He let himself in and silently closed the door behind him. He shook her gently.

'George, wake up,' he whispered.

Nothing. 'George, c'mon. You need to wake up. Th-'

'Wha!' Georgie sat bolt upright.

'Sssh!' whispered Finn. 'It's me. We've got a crisis.'

Georgie rubbed her eyes, focused on Finn. 'What's happened?' she asked groggily.

Finn told her about the house on The Palm, about Shaukat. To his relief, she didn't lambast him for going off on his own. Her concern was for Shaukat.

'I've got a plan,' said Finn. 'We need Fred. Either we *Travel* there, or head out over the wall and run.'

'Let's try to *Travel*. I think I can do it this time,' said

Georgie, rushing into her bathroom, pulling on jeans and a tee shirt. She sat back on her bed and pulled on her red Converse trainers. 'I really do.'

They held hands, each visualising Fred's room with its map-bedecked walls, its balcony with the telescope pointing towards the heavens.

They stayed stuck in Georgie's room. Georgie released Finn's hand, tried on her own. Still she stayed rooted to her bedroom floor.

'Plan B,' said Finn, anxiously checking his watch.

'Can you make your way to Fred's parents boat? Sneak past security, hide on board, wait for us there?'

Georgie nodded. 'It's only a quarter of a mile away. I can jog there quickly.'

'Don't attract attention to yourself,' urged Finn. 'We don't want the police stopping to investigate why a girl is out running on her own at ten thirty at night.'

'I won't.'

Finn gave her a brief hug. 'Oh, I nearly forgot. We need heavy duty masking tape, a chisel and a hammer.'

'I'll get them from the garage.'

Georgie gathered up her backpack. Together they tiptoed to Finn's bedroom. Finn opened his window and watched Georgie climb down the acacia tree.

Finn closed his eyes, focused on Fred's bedroom and jumped.

Fred, reading in bed, bit back a wail when Finn landed in the middle of his bedroom.

'Finn! What's going on?'

'We need your dinghy,' whispered Finn, glancing at realms of hieroglyphics strung out on Fred's bed. 'Now.'

Fred grinned. 'All right. Let's go. You can tell me why

on the way. Just tell me we're not setting sail for Bone Island and the Dark Kingdom again.'

'No. Palm Island. Come on. Can you *Travel?*'

'I can try,' replied Fred determinedly. 'Just let me get some kit on. Don't fancy going out in me jammies.'

Finn grinned, felt a wave of warmth and admiration for his friend. Fred, who had once been so nervous, so shy, was as ready a LightFighter as any of them.

Fred changed into jeans and tee shirt, slipped his feet into trainers, grabbed his backpack, shoved his torch inside it. 'Right. I'm ready. We land on the inside eating area of the boat. The table's retracted, so just *See* the carpet.'

'It's purple flecked with gold, isn't it?' asked Finn.

'Yep, gaudy and memorable,' said Fred, 'thank goodness.'

The two Lightfighters stood side-by-side, silent and focusing. Simultaneously, they disappeared.

CHAPTER THIRTY

Away to Sea
In A Dinghy

EORGIE HURRIED THROUGH THE backstreets, the hammer and chisel clinking gently in her backpack. Mercifully, no police cruisers passed her. A couple of cars did, but the drivers were too pre-occupied to bother about a young girl out alone on the streets.

She slowed as she approached DOSC, the Dubai Off-shore Sailing Club. Marching past the security booth would not be so easy. She huddled down beside a parked car and watched for signs of the guard. She was rewarded after five agonisingly long minutes. The door to his booth clicked open and he headed off into the club.

Georgie walked briskly past his booth, deeper into the grounds of the club. She walked past the club house, forcing herself not to hurry, just trying to look like someone out for a stroll.

She saw the guard off to the right, checking something on the little beach. She walked onto the pontoon. A couple came off one of the boats, walking arm in arm. Georgie sped up so that she passed the end of their pontoon before they got to it. She felt their eyes on her back, half expected them to call out, but they stayed blessedly silent.

She saw Fred's boat now. She headed up to it, jumped lightly across the dock and onto the decks of *Alison*. A door creaked behind her. Georgie let out a yell.

'Ssh, George, it's us,' whispered Finn, beckoning from the stateroom with Fred. Footsteps sounded on the pontoon.

'I say, is everything all right?' asked a voice.

Finn, Fred and Georgie froze, ducking down silently.

'Meeeoooow,' mewed Georgie, tentatively.

'Hello!' said the voice, getting closer. 'Meeeeeeee-aaaaaaaooooouuuuuw,' snarled Georgie. There was silence for long, agonising seconds.

'Cats!' said a dismissive voice. Footsteps retreated away from them and they gave a collective sigh of relief.

'Phew, that was close,' whispered Georgie

'Always thought you looked a bit feline,' said Fred.

'Inspired,' whispered Finn, grinning. His face sobered quickly. 'Let's give that guy five minutes to disappear, then let's get the dinghy going.'

'Engine's attached,' said Fred. 'I've got the key. Here's two flares and matches. Remind me to re-supply when we get out of all this.'

Finn nodded. 'Will do.'

The moon glistened on the water as they waited. Laughter from the clubhouse wafted through the air. For some people, it was an idyllic night. For others, thought Finn, it was hell.

'C'mon. Let's go,' he whispered. They slid into the dingy, released it from *Alison*, unleashed the oars and gently paddled out to sea.

Once they were about two hundred yards off shore, they turned on their light, switched on the engine, and puttered up the coast towards The Palm. Georgie and Finn synchronised their watches, agreed, to the exact second, the timing of their attack.

Ten minutes later, they switched off their light and engine, and rowed down between two fronds.

'I hope this is the right one,' worried Finn. He gazed through the night, scrutinising the houses staring back majestically at him.

'Yes! That's it. That blue and white one down there,' he said pointing. 'This is as close as I think we should get.'

Fred nodded. 'I'll keep the dinghy here. You two go and do your stuff. Good luck.'

'Good luck yourself,' replied Georgie, as she slid into the water beside Finn.

CHAPTER THIRTY ONE

∽ Rescue ∽

THEY SWAM QUIETLY TO shore, Finn holding the flares and matches wrapped in a plastic bag aloft above the water. They waded out of the sea and hurried to the back of the house.

Finn handed the flares to Georgie, took her backpack containing masking tape, hammer and chisel and slung it on.

'When I signal, go to the front of the house and let off the flares, then get the heck back to the dinghy,' he whispered.

'What about you? You can't carry Shaukat alone.'

'George, please,' begged Finn.

'OK. OK. I'm gone.'

Finn hauled himself up onto the balcony and peeked through the window. Shaukat was lying on the bed, apparently asleep. Possibly unconscious. Finn took out the masking tape and taped an area of the window about two feet square. He turned, saw Georgie watching him and gave her the thumbs up.

Georgie gave him one back, then skirted round the garden to the front of the house.

She checked her watch, waited until the exact second agreed with Finn, then struck a match, ignited both flares, threw them about twenty feet into the street. They exploded with a satisfying bang and a pair of brilliant orange plumes rocketed up to the sky. Georgie rushed back round the house and hid in a bush to wait for Finn.

She glimpsed Finn disappearing through the hole he had smashed in the window.

Shaukat lurched to his feet. Finn grabbed him and cut through his bindings.

'Run, can you run?' Finn whispered as shouts broke out downstairs.

Shaukat nodded, grimacing as he moved. Stiff and injured, he hobbled as fast as he could, pulled along by Finn.

'Jump down to me,' urged Finn, vaulting the balcony and dropping to the ground, landing on all fours. Shaukat awkwardly swung a leg over the balcony, then another, then plunged down to the ground. Finn half caught him, but the man's weight threw them both to the ground. Finn jumped up, hauling Shaukat with him. He heard voices shouting from the front of the house. He dragged Shaukat, agonisingly slowly, towards the beach. If the voices came round to the back of the house, they would all be caught. Somehow they would have to stand and fight.

Finn heard a movement behind him. A man appeared. He saw Finn and Shaukat, opened his mouth to shout when Georgie barrelled out of her bush and ran into him. She hit him low, knocked him over. He grunted in surprise as he fell. There was a sickening smack as his head hit the side of a huge metal flowerpot. Finn glanced down at him without pity. He was one of the men who had been kicking Shaukat.

'Let's get out of here,' hissed Georgie, grabbing Shaukat's arm in hers, bearing some of his weight. Finn grabbed his other arm and between them, they hauled him across the garden, down across the sand and into the water.

'Swim!' Finn hissed at Georgie. 'Get to the boat. I'll take Shaukat.' He didn't wait for argument, simply hauled Shaukat onto his back and kicked out with all his might. He needed all his powers now. He summoned them, felt them flooding through his muscles. He slammed his arms through the water, dragging Shaukat's weight as if he were a child, not a man, and a heavy one at that. He swam so fast, he overtook Georgie who was swimming fast herself. He got them to the boat.

'Give me your hand,' urged Fred in a fierce whisper. Shaukat limply extended his arm to Fred. Fred grabbed and pulled while Finn got beneath him and pushed him up. Shaukat moaned and grimaced in agony as his broken ribs were hauled up against and over the edge of the boat. Finn pulled himself in then grabbed Georgie and hauled her in.

Fred grabbed one oar, Finn another and together they pulled through the water, straining every sinew as they moved away from the brightly lit shallows into deeper water.

Georgie sat looking back to the house. Loud shouts boomed across the water, rising to a crescendo of fury.

'They must've discovered Shaukat's missing,' said Georgie. The boat was now in the mid-channel between fronds. Clouds scudded across the moon, veiling them then exposing them.

'There's a boat over there,' said Georgie, pointing to a large white cabin cruiser close to the opposite frond. 'Let's get behind that. It's our only hope. If they come to the beach they'll see us. They're bound to have a speedboat somewhere and they'll be on us in minutes.'

They changed direction, arrowed towards the boat. Georgie peered into the night, eyes fixed on the brightly lit house and the sand before it, expecting, dreading the Dark-Fighters to turn up at any minute.

Finn and Fred hauled on the oars, trying to guide the dinghy round to the back of the boat. One oar got stuck and they bashed into the boat. Cursing, they edged away and round to the far side.

Georgie bent down to Shaukat who was lying prone on the floor of the boat.

'*It's you!*' he shouted.

Finn clamped a hand over his mouth. 'Quiet,' he hissed. 'You'll give us away.'

A roar of boat engines split the night. They all froze.

'Here they come,' said Finn. 'Get down, lie down, don't move, don't speak.' He grabbed the dinghy's rope, threw it over the anchor securing the cabin cruiser.

'Hopefully they'll think the dinghy belongs to the cruiser,' he whispered, flattening himself next to the others on the floor.

The speedboat roared round the frond, screeched past the cabin cruiser and the dinghy, rocking them violently. The engines quietened abruptly as the boat slowed, turned, and headed back their way.

'Let's have a closer look,' said a voice, low with menace. The Policeman!

Finn glanced at Shaukat. He had begun to tremble violently. *Stay calm,* Finn urged him silently. The boat got nearer still. Shaukat trembled even more.

'Can't see anything,' said a different voice.

'Where in hell's name have they gone?' asked The Policeman.

'Reckon they're hiding on the frond somewhere, p'raps in someone's garden,' said another voice. 'There're enough empty houses on the Palm.'

'Would have heard a motor boat,' said a third voice, adding: 'They'd hardly come and snatch the prisoner in a rowing boat.'

There was silence for a few moments before The Policeman spoke again, all the while his boat drifted ever nearer the dinghy.

'All right, let's search the houses on our frond. I'll put on my uniform, get entry into every single one if I have to.'

With a ferocious roar, the engines of the speedboat kicked into life. It reversed away from the dinghy, spun round and headed back to the other frond, a plume of water billowing out behind it.

'Phew, that was close,' said Georgie.

Shaukat gave a moan of relief.

'Let's wait ten minutes, then head back to base,' said Finn. 'In the meantime, Shaukat, tell us everything you know about these men.'

'Evil. They are evil,' replied Shaukat with a shudder. 'They would have killed me, had you not rescued me. They hunt you three. I think they want to kill you too.'

CHAPTER THIRTY TWO

Slow Boat
to India

FRED HAD NEVER BEEN so happy to see Dubai Off-
shore Sailing Club. They moored the dinghy beside
Alison, climbed aboard and attacked the boat's emer-
gency provisions. Several bottles of water, one packet of
crisps and a half tube of Oreo biscuits later, they sneaked
past the slumbering security guard and out onto the streets.
Shaukat was a little stronger after food and water but he
winced in pain with every step. It took them twenty five
minutes, twice as long as usual, to reach the lock-up garage
where Finn, Fred and Georgie kept their quad bikes.

'Sleep here,' said Georgie to Shaukat, making up a
bed for him from camping mattresses. Shaukat sat down
carefully.

'Rest, get stronger, then get the heck out of here,' said
Finn, giving him water and extra provisions from the boat.

'Have you got your passport?' asked Fred.

Shaukat shook his head. 'The men, they have it.'

'You *have* to get out of Dubai,' said Finn.

'I know that,' answered Shaukat. 'I have a friend, he's
a ship's captain. I happen to know he's sailing for India
tomorrow with a cargo. He'll let me on board. I'll get to
India, disappear there. In my country, they won't find me.'

Don't bet on it, thought Finn. 'Good,' he said.

'We'd better get home,' said Fred. 'It'll be dawn soon.'

'Good luck,' said Georgie, shaking Shaukat's hand.

He got painfully to his feet and thanked the three of them profusely. 'You have saved my life, you three children. I owe you my life,' he added, falteringly.

'Look after yourself,' said Finn.

'Get home safely,' said Fred.

'You too,' replied Shaukat. 'What will you do, about those men? They will hunt you until they find you. You must hide.'

'Or fight,' replied Finn.

CHAPTER THIRTY THREE

⚭ Sports' Day ⚭

'WAKE UP FINN. IT'S Sports' Day today,' said a voice that sounded like Aunt C. Finn closed his eyes tighter. He was dreaming. It was the middle of the night.

The Aunt C of his dream began to shake his shoulder. 'Middle of the night,' mumbled Finn. 'Leave me 'lone.'

'Finn, it's six forty five and you need to get up and get dressed in your sports kit or you'll be late.'

Finn sat up. He rubbed his eyes, staring in disbelief at his bedside clock.

'Urgggh,' he croaked, slumping back on his pillows.

'I hope you're not sickening for something,' said Aunt C, feeling his forehead. 'First Georgie refusing to get out of bed, then you too.'

'Temperature's normal.' She frowned at him suspiciously.

'I'm fine,' said Finn quickly. He knew that look, knew it presaged an inquisition. He sat up and swung his feet onto the floor. Groggily he stood up.

'Coffee, toast and I'll be up and at 'em,' he said attempting a grin.

'Hmmm.' Aunt C's suspicious voice followed him down the stairs.

Finn found Georgie in the kitchen. Wordlessly she poured him a mug of coffee and sugared it. Finn added an extra cube for good measure. He gulped down a few mouthfuls, eyes closed in bliss.

He opened them and looked at Georgie.

'You OK?' he asked.

'Mm,' she answered. 'You?'

'Fine. Looking forward to seeing Shamal and Hareb. Have a feeling we'll need to accelerate things.'

'Accelerate what?' asked Aunt C coming up behind them.

'Accelerate,' replied Finn quickly. 'In the hundred meters.'

'Hmmm,' answered Aunt C again, eyes narrowed in scrutiny. The special alarm bell possessed only by mothers was ringing loudly.

CHAPTER THIRTY FOUR

∽ Fast as the Wind ∽

FINN, FRED AND GEORGIE grouped together in
their house colours – red for Camels.

'That's a piece of luck,' said Fred, as Shamal
appeared beside them sporting his red cap.

'Just Saw red,' replied Shamal, 'as Miss Finity was
debating with herself which house to put me in. Something's happened, hasn't it?' he asked, tilting his head on
one side quizzically.

'Hundred meter sprint,' said Georgie, reading the
programme. 'That's Butthead's event. Yes. Something has
happened.'

Shamal gave a soft smile. 'Butthead's event, is it?' The
smile faded. 'Tell me when this carnival is over. We can
meet under your Acacia tre– ah!' Shamal jumped as a voice
boomed out like thunder.

'Welcome everybody! I am delighted to open the twen-
tieth annual Sports' day at the Jumeirah Academy of Music,'
shouted Mr Odey, JAM's new Deputy Head. Finn winced
as the bombastic voice thudded on, amplified horribly by
the sound system.

'Oh shut up Odious,' he muttered, 'and let us get on
with it.' He didn't like the new Deputy. The man looked

like a bully and behaved like one. He was tall, bald-headed, with an extravagant beer belly. He fawned over the sons and daughters of rich and powerful parents while treating everyone else with thinly-veiled contempt.

'I am going to hand over to Miss Finity who will co-ordinate today's races. May the best man win, ha, ha,' thundered Mr Odey before handing over the microphone.

'Thank yu Mr. Odey,' she muttered briskly. 'Raight thairn. Wud the following pupils line up for the first heat,' she called out in her rasping Scottish accent.

'Shaheel Sultan, Brian Bovis, Vlad Czarovich, Andrew Minkin, Walter Ratchett, Mahmoud Lalvani and Soren Peterson.'

Butthead elbowed past, knocking into Shamal.

'Look where you're going, Moron,' snapped Butthead, as if the collision had been Shamal's fault.

Finn opened his mouth to remonstrate but Shamal laid a hand on his arm.

'Leave him. He's not worth it.'

Finn glowered at Butthead's back, then turned to Shamal.

'Good luck,' he said, thinking of how just two short days ago Shamal had writhed on the floor, half dead under Typhon's attack. Shamal, because of the quiet power that radiated from him, appeared much bigger than he was. Now, standing between Butthead and Vlad, a good six inches shorter than them, he looked slight, almost frail.

The rest of the seven runners lined up. Butthead grinned at his fellow competitors, and gave them a wink as if to say: *eat dirt, losers.*

Vlad glared at him. Shamal ignored him. He stood limply, waiting.

'On yer marks, gairt set. Goooo!' yelled Miss Finity.

No-one who saw the race could ever describe it afterwards. All the observers and participants alike could say was that the race started, the boys began to run, and there was a blur of motion, of arms pumping and legs running so fast it was not possible to see them. All they knew was that Shamal came first, the rest nowhere. The other competitors seemed barely to have started when Shamal streaked across the finishing line.

The spectators watched in stunned silence. For once, even Mr Odey was lost for words. He watched, mouth agape. For a few moments, no-one spoke, then the applause started slowly, and built like rising thunder.

Fred clapped dementedly.

Finn watched Shamal, awe-struck.

'He ran like the wind,' said Georgie softly.

'Didn't he,' replied Finn, recalling Shamal's father's words with a frown of worry: *stay safe in the world.* Zephyr had said. *Veil yourself. The world of man does not welcome those who are different, who do not fit the narrow mould.* Finn knew the wisdom of that well enough himself, but he knew too how hard it was to veil yourself, to hold back, and he felt a sudden, fierce bond with Shamal.

Butthead shouldered past him, lumbering after Shamal.

'How'd you run like that?' he demanded, as if it were a personal affront to him. 'How'd you do it?' he added, grabbing Shamal by the shoulder, swinging him round to face him.

Shamal just stared into Butthead's eyes, not saying a word. Butthead shrank back.

'Wierdo!' he said, spitting out the word like a curse.

Shamal turned and walked away. He didn't see Butt-head reach into his pocket, pull out a stone, pull back his arm and throw it at the back of Shamal's head.

But Finn saw. As did one other observer who was watching closely. Finn saw the stone fly with brutal speed. In a fraction of a second it would smash into the back of Shamal's skull. Finn stared at it with all his focus. Abruptly, the stone stopped, centimetres from Shamal's head. It hovered in the air for a second, then reversed its course and hurtled back towards Butthead. Finn directed it at his nose.

Butthead screamed in pain and terror as the stone hit. Blood gushed down his face.

The Policeman's spy watched, a slow smile creasing his lips.

'Got you!' he whispered to himself.

CHAPTER THIRTY FIVE

☙ Unveiled ☙

'SO,' SAID A VOICE by Georgie's ear. 'What's the story there then? Who, or should I say *what* is this new friend of yours?'

Georgie looked up at Vlad. She aimed for a bored shrug.

'How would I know? Just 'cos he beat you.'

Vlad laughed. 'He would have beaten anyone.'

'The rest of you were just slow,' said Georgie. 'Just face it.'

Vlad shook his head. 'I don't think so.'

Miss Finity stared at Shamal. Many eyes watched him, wondering and thinking. The Policeman's spy smiled. He stepped back from the crowd of pupils and tapped out a number on his mobile.

The Policeman answered straight away.

'I have two interesting pieces of information for you. One, there is a new boy here. Not seen him at JAM before. Runs like the wind,' said the spy.

'Ah, really,' replied the Policeman. 'I think I know just who he might be. He would make the perfect gift, give our Master the complete pair. What else?'

'The boy you suspected before, Finn Kennedy. He has

Power.' The spy told the Policeman about the stone.

'Interesting,' mused the Policeman, 'my instincts went on red alert as soon as I clapped eyes on him. I felt his power then. He tried to veil himself, but this time he slipped up.'

'Do you think - '

'That he is the Prince of Atlantis?' cut in the Policeman. 'Our Master suspects him. He felt his power when he pursued him, before he somehow managed to disappear into thin air. Then there's the Prophecy. Three children and a teacher. It was kids who sprung that driver from my house last night. Ashkent saw them before one of them knocked him out. What normal kids could do that, then vanish without a trace, again?'

'Shall I snatch him? He and the runner?'

'What, with a crowd of parents and other teachers around?' barked the Policeman contemptuously.

'There's always a moment when no-one is watching, if you wait long enough, especially for someone in my position. No-one would ever suspect me.'

'Perhaps not, but just watch them for now. See where they go, who their friends are. Stick to them like glue.'

'Will do,' replied the spy.

CHAPTER THIRTY SIX

∞ Triton ∞

FINN AND GEORGIE HEADED for the beach at five. Aunt C had scrutinised them like a hunting hawk when they made their request, but, under Johnny's influence, she had allowed them to go. Finn took his surfboard. He knew from the wind that the waves would be good.

Georgie strolled along the beach while Finn surfed. The waves were too big for her to consider joining him. There were no other children in the water, just a few adults, surfing alongside Finn, casting surprised glances at him as he rode the biggest waves with daring and skill.

Finn whooped with joy as he caught a particularly large wave that roared into the shore. As the sun began to set and a crimson pool bled across the darkening sky, he reluctantly left the waves. He towelled himself dry, pulled on shorts and a tee shirt just as Fred arrived.

Georgie joined them, pulled out a flask from her backpack.

'Tea?' she asked.

Finn shivered, suddenly chilled. 'Love a cup,' he said eagerly.

The three of them sipped their tea as darkness fell and the beach emptied.

Cups drained, they headed up the beach towards the promontory beside the fishermen's village. The waves were too big to go out onto, so they stood by the water's edge.

Triton, they called in their minds. *We need you. Come. Please come.*

They waited in silence in the deepening night. Minutes passed. The moon rode up over the horizon, silvering the breaking waves.

Over and over again they invoked the Sea Djinn of the Light, calling him to them, each of them yearning to see him.

Finn stiffened. He peered out into the churning water, close to the rocks.

'He's there!' he exclaimed. Georgie and Fred squinted into the darkness then they too saw him. First his face, seemingly cast of bronze like a Michelangelo sculpture, all regal planes and an air of eternity. Then his arms and chest rose out of the water, huge muscles gleaming in the wash of moonlight. He gazed about him, then when he was sure no-one else was near, the great Sea Djinn swam towards them. He came to rest in the shallows, coiling his massive dolphin's tail to his side, holding himself up with his arms.

He inclined his head and smiled at the three of them and the warmth of his power and his goodness flowed into them like a benediction.

'Greetings my old friends,' he said, his voice low and musical and rich with time.

'Hello Triton,' they answered in chorus, smiling in pure joy, bowing back.

'Your faces are marked by battle,' observed the Sea Djinn, studying them carefully, 'Tell me. What ails you and your world?'

Quickly, glancing round to make sure no-one else appeared on the beach, they told Triton of the trip to the Empty Quarter and all that had ensued.

Triton listened in silence, his green eyes darkening. He looked to the stars, glinting implacably above.

'Typhon has waited a long time for this war with Zephyr. Now you are part of it. He knows you exist. He will not take the risk that the Travellers' Prophecy will come true and that you will make him disappear. You are in grave danger, Finn. The gravest. He will try to kill you. He and his Policeman.'

Triton turned to Fred and Georgie. 'And you two, by your association with Finn, and in your own right because you are both referred to in the Prophecy, are in mortal danger too.'

Georgie shuddered.

Fred looked grimly ahead.

'He is a true and terrifying adversary, the Dark Storm Djinn,' added Triton.

'And Zephyr?' asked Finn.

'A powerful ally, but do not forget, he is a Djinn of the Wind. He twists and he turns in a moment, this way and that.'

'You mean we cannot trust him?' asked Georgie.

Triton paused. 'No, I do not say that. He is of the Light, but his nature is volatile. He can move faster than you can think, and he can out-manoeuvre anyone.'

'Not you,' said Fred, a question in his eyes.

'Possibly. Over the centuries, he will have done so, probably so well that I shall not even have noticed. Tread carefully with him. Trust your instincts. And be careful of his son, too. I have heard of the boy Shamal. I have seen him, once. He glitters like the starlight that made him. He rescued you all. You owe him the debt of life. He is a beguiling friend. And he is noble, pure of heart, but he is tormented too. He loves his mother and his sister fiercely. He would do anything to free them from their respective imprisonments. Remember that.' He turned to Finn. 'You have a plan, my Prince of Atlantis? I see it gleaming in your eyes.'

'We do.' Finn took a deep breath. 'Part One. We steal the Talismans. Do a trade. Get Typhon to free Mistral. Then, Part Two. Hand over the Talismans and trap Typhon.'

'How?' asked Triton.

Finn smiled and told him.

Chapter Thirty Seven

⚮ Mortal Peril ⚮

RITON CHUCKLED, THE SOUND like water flowing over pebbles.

'Audacious. Brilliant. If you can bring it off….'
He gazed up at the stars again. When he looked back at them his eyes were grave.

'You three LightFighters have triumphed not once, but twice. Each time against the most overwhelming odds. Each time the battle gets harder. Hydrus was sick. Jehannem was a Djinn in full possession of his powers, but Typhon is so much older than him, so much more powerful. Every second of every day you are all in mortal peril. You must execute your plan with all haste. You must strengthen yourselves.'

'How?' asked Fred.

'Dig into your souls. See the Powers that you need. Allow no room for doubt, or hesitation. Think out your plans with all the brilliance you possess then be bold. Harness your courage.'

At that, the Sea Djinn reached out, took first Fred's hand, then Georgie's. They both felt the flood of power, so strong this time they jolted with it.

'Go, now, you two,' he said to them. 'Go to your homes. Go to your beds, rest, then tomorrow you must go in all haste with your friend Shamal to the Castle of the Winds, to Zephyr's protection. You must operate from there.'

He turned to Finn. 'Stay with me a while. There is something you must do.'

CHAPTER THIRTY EIGHT

☙ Force-field ☙

TRITON WATCHED FRED AND Georgie disappear into the night. He turned back to Finn, eyes still grave.

'Hold your hand over your arm, just a few inches above the skin,' he instructed.

Finn did as he was bidden.

'What do you feel?' asked Triton.

'Well, not much really, to be honest.'

'Try again. Use your senses, sharpen your awareness.'

Finn hovered his hand up and down his bare arm. 'Well, I feel warmth.'

Triton nodded. 'Energy.'

'Yes, body heat I suppose.'

'How far out does it reach?'

Finn moved his hand up and down. 'A few inches.'

'Expand it.'

'How?'

'Visualise it extending further from your body. Harness your energy and propel some of it outwards.'

Finn concentrated fiercely, raising his hand up and down to feel the boundaries of the heat which flowed from him.

'I'm not sure I'm getting anywhere,' he replied, frowning in frustration. 'Perhaps I've pushed it out a fraction.'

'I believe that when you were down in Jehannem's Fire Ark, when the whole cursed structure was crumbling and you were plunged into darkness, you expanded your energies rather well,' observed Triton.

Finn remembered the dreadful, enfolding, claustrophobic darkness of the tomb. 'I made light. I made light pour from my body.'

'As you do in the Cave of Light.'

'So do I make light now?'

'No, not light. Think of it as atmosphere, creating your own bubble of energy, of air around you.'

'And I'll be able to feel that?' asked Finn.

'Yes, you'll be able to feel it.'

Finn remembered his lessons from Mr Violet. He slowed his breathing, focused his eyes on a distant point out to sea, conjured his powers from deep inside him.

Gradually at first, then more strongly, heat began to flow up through his body. Finn held onto it, harnessed it, then visualised it leaving his body and hovering around it like a bubble. Tentatively, he reached out to touch his arm. He yelped in surprise.

'It's there! I can feel something. It's warm, it's slightly squashy, like I'm pushing against a tent wall. I feel like I could push through if I had to, but there's a wall there.'

Triton smiled. 'Well done. Now, make it bigger, imagine filling it with the air around you, then imagine sealing it with a membrane, like a tent, but stronger.'

Finn blew out a breath, then slowly sucked in air, drew it to him, imagined it surrounding him, sealing it in with something like plastic. Bullet-proof plastic, he thought to himself. Something that would bend, but not break. He trembled with the effort. It was thrilling, this new power, but harnessing it felt like he was digging around in his bone marrow, grabbing at the very essence of himself.

He reached out, felt for a boundary. It was there! Further away than before, perhaps eighteen inches out.

Triton reached out his great hand, felt the boundary and smiled.

'Very good, Finn. You have created your very own force-field. Now hold onto it for a while, carry it with you. And use it.'

'Use it? How?' asked Finn.

'We will swim to the Cave of Light. I believe you will need to take a few breaths on the way. Come on, let's go.'

Finn flung his arms round Triton's back and gulped in as much air as his lungs could carry. He tried to keep his force-field in place, extending around his body as he and the Sea Djinn swam down beneath the churning surface of the waves.

Through the blackness of the ocean they sped. Finn kept his eyes shut tight, revelling in the sensation as the water sluiced past his body. It felt to him as if he had left his land-dwelling body behind, that he was becoming a sea creature. For a long time they stayed down. *Air*, thought Finn suddenly, *I need air*. He and Triton had always been able to communicate telepathically and now Finn waited for the Sea Djinn to respond, but Triton sped on underwater.

Finn's muscles started to burn. His lungs felt as if they would explode. He was going to have to let go, kick for the surface.

'*Please Triton,*' he called in his mind. '*I need air.*'

'Do you?' replied the Sea Djinn.

'*Yes! Now!*' communicated Finn urgently.

Slowly, agonisingly slowly, Triton took them towards the surface. Finn saw spots form before his eyes and he was on the verge of losing consciousness. Finally they broke the surface and Finn desperately gasped in the briny air. He recovered quickly, but he felt a blast of anger that Triton had kept him down so long.

'Save your defiance,' came the Sea Djinn's voice, with unusual sharpness. Abruptly, he dived again, taking them both under.

Five minutes later they arrived at the Cave of Light. Finn slid from Triton's body and waited for the Sea Djinn to hand him the conch from which he could breathe. He felt Triton waving his hand back and forth before his eyes. He opened them and saw the light streaming from the Sea Djinn and from himself. It illuminated the Cave and its pearlescent ceiling with the stalactites daggering down. Triton handed Finn the super-dense meteoric rock that would anchor him underwater and stop him floating up to the ceiling.

Finn looked around for the conch.

'You don't need it,' said Triton, his voice now high with the peal of a dolphin.

'I do!' communicated Finn.

Triton stared at him, eyes blazing. 'You are an Atlantean. Your heritage runs through your veins. Claim it. Believe in it.'

'*I need air!*' communicated Finn, fear spiking his blood. The spots formed again before his eyes as his oxygen-starved brain began to struggle. He had never seen Triton like this; cold, ruthless and unyielding.

'Then breathe from your force-field. You have air around you.'

Finn shook his head. 'I cannot breathe underwater.'
You do in your dreams, said the voice inside his head.

'You will die if you cannot make this leap,' declared the
Sea Djinn. 'If not now, then in the battle which will come.
Your existing powers are not enough to win this time. You
must grow. Use your new ones. *Believe, Finn,*' he urged.
'*Believe. Reach into yourself.*' He took Finn's hands in one
of his own, gripped them hard. Finn felt the jolt of power
pouring from the Sea Djinn into him. He saw the fierce
protectiveness, the will in his eyes.

I do not want to die, Finn thought. *Not here, not now.
Not later, in battle with Typhon.* He gazed into Triton's eyes,
took courage from the faith he saw. Heart pounding, trembling with fear, he opened his mouth and he breathed.

Chapter Thirty Nine

∽ A New Power ∽

H E SAW A BLUE light like refracted sapphires glittering in the sun. His head felt like it was going to explode. The pain was unbelievable. But brief. It faded rapidly and in its place a strange euphoria soared within his soul. Through the light Finn saw Triton regarding him.

'So?' asked the Sea Djinn.

'I'm not dead,' communicated Finn, grinning wildly.

Triton shook his head.

'I can *breathe*,' added Finn, eyes huge with wonder.

Triton smiled back, but his eyes were cautious. 'For a short time. Only ever for a short time, unless....' He paused, looked off thoughtfully into the distance.

'Unless what?' prompted Finn.

'Never mind,' replied Triton bringing his gaze back to Finn. 'With the size of atmosphere, of force field you create, you can only breathe underwater for a short time, perhaps five minutes, perhaps ten. No more than ten, and only rarely, when you really have to. You use a huge reserve of your power extending your aura, filling it, sealing it. When you have done so you will be weak. You must wait to regain your powers.'

Finn nodded.

'Now we must go,' said Triton, releasing Finn's hands. 'Climb on my back. I'll take you to Shell Beach.'

A yearning rose in Finn like a sudden fever.

Triton,' he communicated. 'Can I swim to the surface alone, then swim back holding on to you.'

Triton studied Finn, eyes dancing with thought. He nodded.

'It will take you perhaps five minutes to surface from here. Do not go straight up. Angle your ascent.'

Finn nodded.

'Do you have enough air?' Triton asked.

Finn nodded. 'I think so,' he communicated, praying he was right.

Triton left the Cave first. Finn glanced around at the lustrous mother-of-pearl ceiling, at the dazzling golden light, drawing power from it then he dropped the meteoric stone, kicked for the exit and angled his body through the water.

He swam as he did in his dreams, oscillating up and down, legs clamped together like a tail, arms pinned by his sides. He had to angle up slowly or risk getting the bends. Soon his muscles burned. They needed oxygen. Heart racing, he opened his mouth and he breathed. Enough air, thank the light, thin, running out, but enough. He felt a surge of power, felt a joy like nothing he had ever experienced before.

A minute later, he shot up through the surface back into the world of man.

The moon was high in the sky when they returned to Shell Beach. Finn waded from the water, turned to salute Triton.

'Thank you,' he said, 'for my gift.'

Triton shook his head. 'It was not mine to give. You had it in you all along, you just didn't know it. Now you do, but use it wisely, and rarely. It is intoxicating, Finn. Remember who you are.'

That was just it, thought Finn. Sometimes he wasn't sure anymore. Boy? Prince of Atlantis? LightFighter? Could he be all three at the same time? He shivered in the darkness. There was something the Sea Djinn wasn't telling him and it hovered between them like a ghost.

CHAPTER FORTY

෧ Crunch ෨

F RED AND GEORGIE HAD stopped for hot chocolate and cup cakes at Sugar Daddy on Beach Road. Stomachs groaning, they said goodbye with a wave and headed off to their respective homes. Fred had a sense of unfinished business. There was something useful he could be doing, he was sure of it. He swung through the gate into his floodlit garden and headed in through the kitchen door.

His mother was sitting on a stool beside the marble island, swinging her kitten heels whilst sipping a hot chocolate of her own, something she only did when she was upset.

'Bad for the waistline but good for the soul,' she said brightly. Fred could see she was trying hard to put on a cheerful face, and he loved her for it. She got up and planted a kiss on his cheek

She drew back, holding Fred at arms length, studying him closely.

'What?' asked Fred, puzzled by her scrutiny.

'You're buzzing,' she said slowly. 'It's like I can feel something buzzing through you.'

Fred affected a shrug. It was Triton's power she could feel, surging through him. He glanced at his palm. It was still luminescent. Fred patted her shoulder, deliberately rubbing off some of the luminescence on her. She looked like she could do with it.

She smiled and her face regained its normal determined look.

'Let's go and pick up Daddy, shall we?'

'Yeah, sure,' Fred answered. 'Of course, Mum. But what's wrong with Dad's car?' A horrible thought struck him. 'He hasn't had a crash or anything has he?'

His mother shook her head. 'Just a financial crash, like everybody else.' She paused, blew out a breath. 'His boss, you know, that horrible new man Schmichael who came in two months ago, the Axeman of Pinner they call him. Well, he took your father's company car away today. Said they were cutting back and cars were an unnecessary expense. Your father is gutted,' she added. 'He thinks it's just the first blow, that he'll lose his job. Maybe in days.'

Fred's mother's eyes were full of pain, both for her husband, and for herself, and Fred could see, for him too.

'We'll have to go back to live in Swindon, with my parents if that happens, Fred. We couldn't afford to go on living here.'

Fred felt a riot of emotions. No, that could not happen, for a million reasons that could not be allowed to happen.

'We have to prepare ourselves, Fred,' added his mother, 'but I thought it would be nice to go and pick up Daddy, rather then let him take a cab.'

'Good idea,' said Fred, determinedly cheerful. There had to be a way to save his father's job. It was just a matter of coming up with a plan, and he was good at that. If he could free frozen Fire Djinns, he could figure out a way to save his father's job.

CHAPTER FORTY ONE

A Dangerous
E mail

T HE NASDAQ SCREEN AT DIFC spewed out realms of red as it recorded the latest financial haemorrages leaking around the world. Fred stared at it, as if he might find an answer in the ever-changing numbers.

His mother parked underneath Emirates Towers and together they took the ear-popping lift up to Fred's father's 40th floor office.

It was practically deserted. Offices lay empty, lights turned off. Unseen fingers tapped unseen keyboards, the faintest snatches of conversation drifted through the gloom. Ghost town, thought Fred.

'Hey, Freddie!' called his father, eyes lighting up. 'And Alison. What a sight for sore eyes you both are.' He gave them both a big hug. 'Shall we go?' he suggested.

'So sorry to interrupt this touching scene,' cut in a sarcastic voice. 'Caradoc, I need a word. Boardroom, I think.'

Fred turned his gaze upon the speaker, a gaunt man, armoured with a pin-striped suit of funereal back. He had the pared-down ascetic features of a priest or a marathon runner. He had a gleaming bald pate, rimless glasses which veiled his eyes and shot your own reflection back at you and thin, seemingly bloodless lips. Schmichael, the Axeman of Pinner, thought Fred, taking a violent dislike to the man. He watched his father follow Schmichael, shoulders sagging under the anticipated blow.

'Hideous man,' hissed Fred's mother, lips white.

'Where's Schmichael's office?' asked Fred as an idea crystallised in his mind. 'Quick, Mum, where?'

'Over there, I think,' she answered, pointing. 'Fred, what are you up to?' she whispered.

'Never mind. Just stay here, distract him if he comes back. *Please* Mum.'

Fred's mother paused for a moment. 'All right. Do whatever it is you're going to do, Fred, but make it good, make it quick and don't get caught.'

Fred turned and ran towards the office his mother had pointed out. He glanced around quickly. No-one in sight. He entered the office. Immediately he saw a whole wall covered with blown up photographs of Scmichael shaking hands with important people.

He sat down at Schmichael's desk. 'Bingo,' he thought. The man's computer was switched on, his e mails up on screen. Fingers racing over the keyboard, Fred Googled the Museum of Cairo, wrote down an e mail address on his hand, then went back into Schmichael's e mails and devised an e mail of his own.

'Dear Sirs,

As Senior Partner of Rapid Capital, I have a proposition which I trust you will take most seriously. One of my investment banking clients would very much like to buy Tutankhamen's Book of the Dead which we believe is in your possession at the National Museum of Cairo. I must inform you that my client is an exceptionally wealthy man and an extremely determined one. I trust that we can do business. It would be the most pleasant way forward, and would I believe spare you much unpleasantness, especially in view of your recent loss of Tutankhamen's Ankh in London.

Yours in anticipation,
Desmond Schmichael.

Fred quickly read through the e mail, spell-checked it, took a deep breath and hit SEND just as he heard his mother calling him urgently.

He jumped up from Schmichael's desk, ran from his office, then slowed to a walk and re-joined his mother just as Schmichael rounded the corner with his father.

Schmichael scarcely looked at Fred and his mother and conspicuously failed to say goodnight to Fred's father.

'Sorry to keep you waiting,' said Fred's father with forced cheer. 'Shall we go home now?'

As Fred's mother drove, she quizzed his father.

'What did that nasty piece of work want?'

'He asked me to take a seventy five per cent pay cut. The alternative being to leave,' he added bitterly. 'As if anyone is hiring investment bankers right now.' He rubbed his hands briskly over his face. 'He's given me forty eight hours to think it over.'

'Oh darling.'

'A lot can happen in forty eight hours,' said Fred, considering his e mail and the likely response of the National Museum of Cairo to a threatening missive from the Senior Partner of what was meant to be a reputable investment bank.

Later that night, when his parents were in bed, Fred prepared stage two of his plan. He stole downstairs to his computer that nestled in the den next to the kitchen. He made himself a peanut butter sandwich and a cup of English breakfast tea, heavily sugared. It was going to be a long night.

The computer came to life with a companionable drone. Fred went to Google, called up the National Museum of Cairo again. He took an electronic tour of the museum. Deeper and deeper into the archives he went, down to the architectural drawings of the museum. By four in the morning, he had a pretty good idea of the layout of the place. Exhausted, but satisfied, he finally went to bed.

He dreamt of long, echoing corridors, of ancient artefacts, of The book of the Dead. In his dream, he could feel the ancient binding, the faded papyrus, desiccated and venerable against his fingers.

CHAPTER FORTY TWO

∽ A Spy Watches ∽

THE DAY DAWNED GREY and forbidding. Fred breakfasted quickly, pulled on his winter jersey against a sudden chill and hopped into his mother's car. His father sat in pensive silence beside his mother as she drove.

'Hang on in there, Dad,' said Fred, as his parents kissed him goodbye. Fred's father gave him a sad smile.

'Oh, and er, Dad, avoid Schmichael. Don't answer his question about taking a salary cut.'

'Why not, Fred?' asked Fred's father, eyeing him sharply.

Fred shrugged. 'Just a feeling,' he said. 'Intuition.' He smiled, making his father think of a spider who had just caught itself a very large fly.

'What goes around often seems to come around,' explained Fred.

He left his parents, fervently hoping he was right. He thought of Chaos Theory; a butterfly flaps its wings and empires fall. Perhaps one little e mail could make one small empire fall.

He waited impatiently under the acacia tree. Shamal drifted up to him with a smile, smelling faintly of incense.

There were dark shadows beneath his eyes as if he too had passed a sleepless night.

'Something might happen today. Something useful I mean,' said Fred excitedly. He spotted Finn and Georgie heading towards them. He beckoned them quickly.

'What's up?' asked Finn.

Fred quickly told them about the e mail to the National Museum of Cairo. Shamal watched him speculatively.

'Nice revenge,' said Georgie. 'Wait, it's more than that isn't it?' she said, a huge grinning spreading across her face.

'So you, or rather Schmichael, is threatening to steal the Book of the Dead unless the Museum sells it to him,' said Finn.

Fred nodded.

'And, if they do in fact have the Book of the Dead, then they might move it,' added Georgie.

'And Mistral could see it and tell us where it's hidden. Brilliant!' declared Shamal, clapping Fred on the back.

'Thank you,' said Fred. 'It might also get my father's hideous boss into trouble, or distract him from firing my father.'

'Maybe the horrible Mr Schmichael will get fired himself,' said Georgie fiercely. 'I hope so.'

'I'll have to try to communicate with Mistral,' said Shamal, oblivious to Fred's personal drama.

'And if she can identify where the Book of the Dead is, we Astral Travel there and steal it,' announced Fred.

'Flipping heck,' muttered Georgie. 'This is moving fast.'

'We have to move fast,' said Finn grimly. 'Remember Triton's warning. He pretty much told us to go to the Castle of the Winds today,' he told Shamal. 'He said we are not safe here, in our world.'

Georgie shivered as a sudden breeze chilled her skin.

Shamal nodded. 'I think he's right. My father told me the same. The Policeman will be back for sure. He knows where to find us. He can lead Typhon to us. Let's talk to Hareb, as soon as class is over. Then go to the Castle of the Winds and - '

The bell shrilled, cutting off Shamal's words. Grim faced, they headed for their class.

Cold eyes watched them pass just feet away, so close he could have reached out and grabbed them.

CHAPTER FORTY THREE

❧ Typhon Returns ❧

THE NEXT LESSON WAS science and by some weird co-incidence, Hareb had decided to talk about Chaos Theory. He was just a quarter of the way through his lesson when he paused and looked uncertainly out of the window.

Finn followed his glance, saw the dark storm clouds massing. He swore under his breath. *Please, please, let it be the weather, just the weather, not Typhon.*

Hareb shook his head, as if throwing something off, then continued his lesson. Outside, the wind picked up. The windows rattled as a gust slammed into them. The door burst open. Mr Odey blew in on a gust of wind.

'Shaheel Sultan,' he called out officiously. 'Come with me. There's someone waiting to see you in Reception.'

Shamal glanced in puzzlement at the man, but he rose slowly to his feet. The windows bulged alarmingly as another gust of wind hit them. Finn could see the palm fronds outside lilting madly under the onslaught. Even inside, with the windows shut, they could hear the roar of the wind. It sounded, thought Finn, like an animal; a hungry, hunting animal. Alive and voracious.

Hanging on threads around their necks, Triton's sea

glass pendants turned dark and gave out a pulse that felt like pain. Finn reached for his, saw the colour. He jumped from his seat.

'DarkFighters near,' he hissed to Georgie and Fred.

A thump at the front of the classroom. They all swung round. Hareb lay slumped on the floor.

Finn rushed up to him followed by Georgie and Fred. Unnoticed, Mr Odey took hold of Shamal's hand. 'Come on now, boy. Don't want to keep your very important visitor waiting, do you?'

Shamal tried to yank his hand free. He called out for help, but, just at that moment, the wind shattered the windows, showering the students with a thousand fragments of glass, filling the room with screams of terror.

Fred peered out through the gap, framed by jagged shards. 'The Dark Meniscus!' he yelled.

Finn nodded, bending over Hareb as if to shield him. Hareb convulsed violently. Finn felt frantically for a pulse. He found it, but it was desperately weak. Finn felt the force of Typhon, the dark magnetism, like the presence of a Black Hole. It seemed to be sucking the life out of Hareb. He glanced around. He had no choice, no matter that the other pupils might see him. Sitting amidst the shards of broken glass, the wind whipping papers through the air in a demented fury, Finn called up his powers. He spread his hands above Hareb's body. Light flooded from him and spread out like a blanket of air over the teacher. Finn visualised the boundary. He dug down into himself, he tried to push it out further, to cover Georgie and Fred and some of the other students who cowered nearby, hiding under desks, faces ribboned with blood from the flying glass.

Outside, the wind screamed in bestial fury. Finn and his force-field reeled as the demonic pull of the dark magnetism switched onto him. He felt as if his organs would be pulled out from his skin. He fought back, calling desperately on the Light, but he was tiring now and his force-field began to shake. Darkness clouded his vision. He felt it beginning to fill his body. The edge of unconsciousness licked at him like dark fire. In the distance, he heard the boom of thunder.

The thunder roared again, directly overhead. Finn felt the wind hammering into his body, into his heart. The darkness rose in a horrific surge. Finn felt it rising, ever higher. He was drowning, drowning...

CHAPTER FORTY FOUR

A Useful
Hockey Stick

F RED RIPPED HIS EYES off Finn's body. Finn was
dying. He could see that. Georgie had grabbed his
hands. She was trying to Astral Travel with him to
get him away, and failing. She was calling out to him: *Hang
in there, Finn. Stay with us, stay with us!* But Fred could see
him slipping away. He glanced round wildly. Where was
Shamal? He must be able to help, to summon his father,
or perhaps to push Typhon away. Why had he disappeared,
now of all times?

Then Fred remembered. Mr Odey! He had appeared,
called out to Shamal, just when the sea glass pendants
turned dark. The Deputy Head was a DarkFighter!

Fred sprinted for the door, crunching the glass shards
underfoot, leaping over the bodies of pupils cowering from
the wind.

'Shamal!' he screamed. Where would he go, Mr Odey?
Where would he take Shamal? On instinct, Fred ran towards
his office. He would need a weapon. What could he use?
P.E. Department. Stores. He ran in, grabbed a hockey stick,
ran out. One more corner. Mr Odey's office. Fred burst in,
saw Mr Odey binding Shamal's hands behind his back. Fred
didn't hesitate. He brought up the hockey stick, crashed it

down on Mr Odey's head. The man screamed, staggered backwards and fell to the floor. Fred grabbed Shamal.

'Run!' he screamed, as Shamal tore at the bonds on his arms. 'Typhon is killing Finn and Hareb. In the classroom. Run!'

Shamal moved. In a blur of legs, he disappeared.

Chapter Forty Five

❧ A Time to Flee ❧

S HAMAL SCREECHED TO A halt beside Finn's and Hareb's prone bodies. A miasma of Dark Energy rose from them.

'Father, come, please, come. Zephyr, King of the Winds, in the name of Light, come,' he called.

Seconds passed. Georgie stayed bent over Finn. Puffing like a sprint racer, Fred rushed in and joined her.

Outside, the wind screamed anew. The clouds scudded away as a new wind stormed in, blowing everything from its path.

Zephyr blew straight at Typhon. Together the winds raged. Spinning, colliding, they tore into whirlwinds that sucked up cars, flinging them like pebbles through the air.

Zephyr called on his powers, blasted the sky with Light. Typhon was tiring. Light, there was too much Light. This was a battle he would finish when he had the Talismans.

With a screech, he turned, and, as abruptly as he had blown in, he blew away. With Typhon gone, Zephyr reined in his power. The wind fell. The roaring ceased. Tormented leaves fell to the ground. The pupils and teachers, cowering in JAM, slowly sat up.

Finn lay prone, but somewhere, far, far away came a voice:

'Come back, Finn', called the voice. *Come back to us'!*

In the deepest recesses of his mind, in his last few breaths, Finn heard the voice. Arms and legs, sucked almost lifeless flailed in the black tide. '*Fight!'* screamed the voice.

Georgie's voice, coming from far away, but so insistent. Finn kicked. He fought, he felt himself drift up a bit. Up he came, slowly, so slowly, like a deep diver, inch by inch pushing back the blackness.

His eyes flew open. He pushed himself up. Georgie fell upon him. 'Finn! You're alive. Thank God!' she shouted. Fred fell to his knees and grabbed Finn in a bear-hug.

'Had us worried for a bit there,' he said, face ashen.

Finn gave a grim smile. He turned to Hareb. Their friend and teacher lay prone, eyes open, filled with horror as if staring at some sight invisible to the others. Georgie grabbed his wrist, searching for a pulse.

'Alive,' she said. 'But weak as anything.'

'He's in a coma,' said Shamal, his voice a rasp. 'Just like my mother.'

Finn flinched suddenly. He reached under his shirt. 'Look. The Sea Glass is turning dark again. DarkFighters coming.'

'It'll be Odious!' shouted Fred. 'He's a DarkFighter.'

Finn struggled to his feet, turned to Shamal. 'We need to get to the Castle of the Winds. *Now!'*

Shamal nodded.

Finn grabbed Hareb's shoulders. Georgie and Fred took hold of his legs. Shamal held Hareb's back.

'Let's get him into the corridor where no-one can see us,' said Finn. Watched by bemused pupils, they carried

Hareb out into the deserted corridor. The sea glass pendant throbbed against Finn's chest.

'We have to hurry,' he whispered, fear hollowing his stomach.

'Think of the Castle. There's a Safe Room, lined with gold,' intoned Shamal.

Georgie screamed as Mr Odey rounded the corner at a run, followed by a tall thin man and by the Policeman.

They were ten feet away and closing fast.

'Focus!' urged Shamal, closing his eyes to them. 'Stay with me. Hold on.'

The men launched themselves through the air in flying rugby tackles. They grabbed Fred, Finn and Georgie, who thudded to the floor breaking the chain. Shamal, clinging desperately to Hareb, disappeared with his teacher.

Chapter Forty Six

☙ Kidnap ☙

FINN, FRED AND GEORGIE were yanked to their feet and marched down the corridor. Finn felt what seemed to be the barrel of a gun against his shoulder.

'Do not attempt to escape. If you do a bullet goes into the back of your skull, and then into your friends. Clear?' growled the Policeman.

'Clear,' hissed Finn, desperately trying to think of a way for them all to escape.

The Policeman forced Finn down the fire escape into the back car park. The rest of them followed close behind. The door to a black Range Rover with heavily tinted windows swung open. The children were pushed into the back seat, forced down onto the floor. Mr Odey and the thin man, whose name seemed to be Ashkent, sat above them, feet pushing into their ribs.

The Policeman jumped into the passenger seat.

'Drive,' he commanded. 'The Palm. Double quick.' He turned in his seat.

'Stay down,' he barked. 'Try anything and you are all dead. Clear?'

'Clear,' they answered. The doors clicked locked and the car sped off, turning onto the traffic of Al Wasl Road, speeding past the familiar landmarks, Park and Shop, Spin-neys, Choithrams. Fred wondered if they would ever see them again.

They arrived at The Palm. The car drove into a garage. Finn, Fred and Georgie were hauled out and dragged into a huge, marble floored room.

'Guard those two until I come back,' the Policeman instructed Odey, gesturing to Fred and Georgie. He walked across to Ashkent, lowered his voice, but Finn heard him whisper: 'Get the boat ready. We'll take them out to sea, shoot them and dump them overboard.'

CHAPTER FORTY SEVEN

∽ A Time to Die? ∽

THE POLICEMAN HEADED BACK to Finn, grabbed his arm and jammed his pistol against his back. 'You and I are going to have a conversation.'

Finn's mind whirred in panic and terror. *Stay calm*, he ordered himself. *It's your only chance.* He could not Astral Travel. He could not leave Georgie and Fred here, waiting to be murdered. He would have to stay and fight, or outwit the Policeman. He slowed his breathing, summoned his powers as the Policeman forced him up a flight of stairs. He was exhausted after Typhon's attack, but fear was a wonderful thing. It flooded his body with adrenalin and energy.

The Policeman opened a door, gestured Finn into a huge bathroom, locked the door behind him. Keeping his pistol trained on Finn, he put the plug in a large sink and turned on the taps.

'You are a Prince of Atlantis. My Master thinks so. I agree with him. You fought him bravely just now. Had to be rescued, of course by the Djinn of the Light,' he spat out the words. 'But you fought. You removed any doubt we might have had about your true identity.'

Finn focused on his force-field, blocking out all else. He extended it around him, pushing it out, hardening the edges.

'The Lord Typhon would like to know how you planned to kill him,' intoned the Policeman. 'So. Speak.'

Finn stayed silent. The Policeman waited.

'Perhaps this will help you find your voice,' he hissed, grabbing for Finn's hair. Finn fought his instincts. He let the Policeman into his force-field, allowed him to grab his hair, allowed him, after a token struggle, to push his head into the sink full of water.

You can breathe, Finn told himself, fighting for calm. *You can breathe.* Slowly, he opened his mouth and he breathed. In came the air, like nectar to a bee, like power. Finn affected to struggle against the Policeman's grip. The man just laughed, tightened his grip.

The seconds passed. Tick, tock, tick tock, breathe, rest, breathe, rest. One minute, two minutes. Finn's head was yanked out of the water. He released his force-field, made a show of gasping in fresh breath. The Policeman pulled back his head and glowered at him.

'Now will you speak?' he demanded.

Finn stayed silent. When he had taken in enough air, he rebuilt his force-field, while still allowing the Policeman in.

The Policeman rammed Finn's head down into the sink again, smashing his forehead into the marble. Finn flinched at the pain, let out a breath, slowly breathed in a new one, pretended to struggle once again. Time slipped by, minute after minute.

The Policeman yanked Finn's head out of the water. Again Finn coughed and gasped, faking a desperation that he was just managing to subdue. The Policeman hauled Finn around so that he was facing him. The man gazed into his eyes. His pupils, Finn noticed, were edged in red, as if he were rabid.

'Now will you speak!' he screamed again at Finn.

Finn shut out the image of the rabid face, saw instead Triton, remembered swimming with him underwater. He released his force-field, sucked in more air, focused his mind.

'Well then, time to die, Prince of Atlantis. No last words?'

Finn re-formed his force-field just before the Policeman smashed his head under water once more. Finn knew he meant to kill him now, that this was not just torture, this was murder. He recognised the thought, then banished it. He kept calm, willed his pulse to stay slow. He faked a struggle, faked giving up when the Policeman slammed his head against the bottom of the sink again. He sipped at the air in his force-field, unsure how long it would last. Minutes passed. Still Finn sipped at his air. He calculated that when three minutes had passed, that should be enough. Slowly, he let his body go limp. He felt the Policeman holding him up. He let his legs collapse. The Policeman took his weight, still holding his head under. Finn felt the air beginning to thin. He rationed himself to tiny sips. Soon, surely, the Policeman would be convinced. Seconds ticked by like minutes. Finn wondered how much air he had left. He slowed his breathing even more, struggled to keep down the rising panic. Finally, the Policeman hauled him from the water, let his body crash to the floor.

Finn lay still, eyes fixed on the marble tiles beneath him, not breathing, not moving, faking death. He felt a blow in his ribs as the Policeman drove a vicious kick into him. He let his body absorb it, bit back the urge to suck in a breath of pain.

'I will keep your body,' announced the Policeman. 'Present it to the Dark Lord as a gift.' He walked from the bathroom, slamming the door behind him.

CHAPTER FORTY EIGHT

❧ Dead as Dodos ❧

F INN LAY STILL, CHEEK pressed against the cold marble, feeling the indentations of the tiles press into his skin. He stayed there, motionless, save the tiny rising and falling of his chest as he took in air.

He heard the Policeman shout out downstairs.

'He is dead, your friend. Dead as a dodo!'

'You pig!' screamed Georgie.

Finn heard a thud and a gasp, imagined the Policeman punching her.

'Leave her alone,' shouted Fred, a low hatred in his voice that Finn had never heard before. Again came the thump. Finn imagined the Policeman's fist colliding with Fred's face. He forced himself to stay still, to breathe, to wait.

'Boat ready?' barked the Policeman.

'Yes, sir,' answered Ashkent.

'Grab the brats and let's go,' replied the Policeman.

Finn waited till he heard the door close. Slowly he got to his feet, raised himself up, peered out of the bathroom window. He saw the Policeman walking arm in arm with Georgie, as if out for a stroll. Mr Odey adopted the same guise with Fred, no doubt in case any of the neighbours happened to be looking their way. Ashkent followed, glancing sharply left and right like a bodyguard.

Finn watched them walk from the lawned back garden onto the jetty that ran out into the water. An inflatable boat stood moored and waiting.

Now, thought Finn. Carefully, he opened the bathroom door, hurried downstairs on soundless tiptoes. Tried a room, got lucky. The kitchen! He saw a chopping board, saw the knife laid out on it, grabbed it. He slunk out of a side door, watched the boat set off slowly, with all the occupants looking forward, away from the house, away from him. Gripping the knife to his side, he sprinted across the grass, down to the jetty. Slowly, he lowered himself into the water, and, knife carried between his teeth, he swam as he had never swum before, faster than in any race, faster than in any dream.

After the boat he went, underwater, breathing in his own air. He swam like the Prince of Atlantis he was. His body felt like a torpedo as it homed in on its target. He surfaced for extra air, saw the boat just twenty metres ahead of him. Soon it would escape the confines of The Palm, pick up speed, roar away into the open water, far from rescue.

Finn lashed his limbs through the water, faster and faster, closer and closer. He felt a sudden throb as the boat's engine powered up. Two more strokes and he was level with the boat. A trailing mooring rope swished into his face. He grabbed it, hung on, hauled himself up, hampered by the knife he grasped in one hand. Up he went, over the side. Georgie and Fred, tied together looked round at him in amazement. He jumped at them, severed the ropes with his knife.

The Policeman screamed in rage and disbelief. 'You! You're dead. I killed you.'

He fumbled in his pocket, drew out a gun, pulled the trigger just as Finn hauled Fred and Georgie down, out of the way. The bullet smashed into the petrol tanks.

Finn grabbed Georgie and Fred. 'Dive!' he screamed. 'It's going to blow!'

Together they leapt over board. Finn pulled them under, kicked with all his strength, going down into the welcoming blackness.

They felt the water roar around them as the petrol tanks ignited, blowing the boat and its occupants into a thousand tiny pieces. Finn held them all down, kicking his legs to keep them under. Seconds later, fragments of metal from the engines daggered into the water. Finn could feel Georgie and Fred struggling, desperate for air. He angled away, fearing the water above them would be aflame with burning oil. He kicked out, dragging Fred and Georgie with him. They kicked too and moments later they surfaced. metres away, the sea burned. Charred remnants of the boat bobbed on the waves. Of Mr Odey, Ashkent, and the Policeman, there was no trace.

CHAPTER FORTY NINE

ᔕ Nowhere is Safe ᔕ

'WE NEED TO GET out of here,' said Finn. 'The coastguard and police'll be here any minute.'

Georgie and Fred trod water, pushing away debris from the boat that floated their way.

'Got my vote,' said Fred. 'Home?' he asked hopefully.

Finn shook his head. 'Nowhere's safe here. Typhon will keep on coming until he's killed us all. We have to go to The Castle of the Winds.'

Georgie and Fred exchanged anguished glances. 'For how long, d'you think?' asked Georgie.

'However long it takes to get the Talismans. Once we have those we can bait the trap with them. That's our only hope of beating Typhon. Of staying alive.'

'I just want to see my parents and the twins, one more time,' said Georgie. She wanted to say her goodbyes, just in case. She bit her lip, eyes fiercely refusing to let fall the tears that suddenly sprang.

Finn nodded, understanding.

'I do too,' added Fred. 'I want to say goodbye to Mum and Dad.'

Finn felt torn. He wanted to say his own goodbyes too. He glanced at the sun.

'The Dark Meniscus is gone. The Policeman's dead, and his cronies, so they won't trouble us. Typhon will assume that they'll have killed us, so that will have bought us a bit of time,' he reasoned. 'As long as no other spies saw the boat blow up and then summon Typhon. Maybe, just maybe we have time. But if we get it wrong, if Typhon tracks me to your house Georgie…'

'Then we're all dead,' she answered, face ashen. 'My parents and the twins too.'

'Fifteen minutes,' said Finn. 'No more. We'll *travel*, do what we have to, then George, we'll *travel* to Fred's bedroom. From there we all go to the Castle of the Winds. For as long as it takes.'

'Deal,' said Fred.

'Done' said Georgie.

CHAPTER FIFTY

∾ A Final Goodbye ∾

FRED FOCUSED ON A thick bush in his garden. There was a perfect hiding space underneath the over-hanging branches. He *Saw* it in his mind, he smelled the flowers, he felt the rough branches. He leapt. And disappeared.

The police sirens screamed ever louder. They were just a few hundred yards away and closing rapidly.

'Let's *See* the storage room in the garage,' said Finn.

'Works for me,' said Georgie.

They grasped hands, *Saw* and *Leapt*. The sea sucked at them and then they were gone.

'Georgie! Finn!' exclaimed Aunt C as they walked into the kitchen.

'Look at you both!' Where have you been? We've been frantic. That shamal! You weren't at school. We were all called, told to come and get you.'

'Crossed wires,' said Georgie. 'We went to Shama- I mean Shaheel's house. His mother picked us up.' She hated lying, but a lie was kinder than the truth.

'But you're hurt! Finn, you've got a huge lump on your forehead and bruises all - '

'Flying debris,' said Finn. He went up and enveloped his Aunt in a huge hug. 'I'm all right. But thanks for caring.'

She hugged him back, touched by his show of affection. Georgie piled in for a hug too. For a moment, she just stood there, tears streaming down her face, relishing the hug, wishing it could last forever. She brushed the tears from her face before her mother saw them, broke free.

'Well,' said Aunt C, patting her hair. 'Go and clean up, then I expect you could do with a meal and an early night. You both look completely whacked.'

They both went through to the sitting room first, found the twins and Johnny sitting together watching a DVD. Georgie slid in between the twins, snuggling them. Then she leaned over and gave her father a huge kiss.

'Glad you got home all right,' he said mildly. 'Bit worried about you.'

'I'm fine. I'll always be fine, Daddy. Don't you worry about me.'

Georgie noted the look of alarm flicker in her father's eyes. She jumped to her feet.

'Gotta clean up,' she said, hurrying from the room.

'Me too,' said Finn, giving them a kind of salute. Any more hugs and Johnny would have become downright suspicious, so Finn contented himself with a smile. He imprinted the three of them on his memory, sitting there, smiling back at him, the love and warmth lighting their eyes. Quickly, he turned and ran upstairs.

Trying to shut off his emotions, Finn wrote one note to Aunt C and Uncle Johnny and another one to his parents, who were off again at sea, near Madagascar, last he'd heard. Quickly, he packed spare clothes and his Swiss army knife in his backpack.

Georgie savagely brushed the tears from her cheeks as she finished writing her note. *I'll be back,* she ended it, swearing to herself that she would be.

She left it lying on her bed, then, with a nervous glance at her watch, at the minutes racing by, she started packing. She grabbed her mini Swiss army knife, a present from Finn, and shoved it down into her backpack pocket. Quickly she packed other essentials; spare clothes, maglite torch, heavy in her hand like a weapon. She added matches and a water bottle. She took a small vial from her bathroom cabinet. Sleeping potion. Mr Violet had shown her how to make it. She had used up all her first batch, but she had made this new one a few weeks ago, acting on some un-named instinct. She wrapped it carefully in tissue paper and slid it into a concealed inner pocket in her backpack.

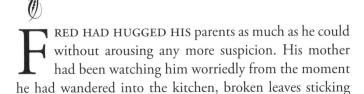

CHAPTER FIFTY ONE

Schmichael Stymied

FRED HAD HUGGED HIS parents as much as he could without arousing any more suspicion. His mother had been watching him worriedly from the moment he had wandered into the kitchen, broken leaves sticking out of his hair.

'Just going to change,' he said after he'd shared a quick cup of tea with his parents.

Upstairs in his bedroom, he wrote his letter, signing it with a promise to return. He laid it on his desk, then, trying desperately to keep his feelings at bay, he gathered up the dictionary of hieroglyphics he had downloaded and his research materials on the National Museum of Cairo and stowed them in his backpack. He checked his watch. Finn and Georgie should be here in four minutes. He sat on his bed and he waited.

A shout from his father made him jump to his feet.

Fred peeked out of his bedroom. His father was talking on his mobile. 'Tell me again,' he urged whomever he was talking to. He listened intently, then he yelled: *'Yes!'* and punched the air. He turned to his wife, standing expectantly beside him.

'Schmichael's been suspended!' he exclaimed. He pointed at his phone. 'Roger's there now. Said Head Office flew in, all very hush-hush, but he overheard something about threats, about a museum, if you can believe that. Anyway, they went through Schmichael's computer and found all this other stuff on it that shouldn't have been there. Long and short of it, he's suspended, pending an investigation.'

Fred smiled to himself. So he *had* helped. His plan seemed to have worked. Whatever pain he was about to inflict on his parents, he had at least managed to protect his father's job. He walked to the window, gazed out. The smile faded from his face. The Dark Meniscus was back. He glanced at his watch. Three minutes till Finn and Georgie were meant to be with him. Three minutes would be too late. He could only pray that they'd seen the Dark Meniscus too.

'*Oh God. Hurry, Finn. Hurry, Georgie*', he whispered, heart contracting with fear.

CHAPTER FIFTY TWO

Narrow Escape

FINN GRABBED HIS BACKPACK and crept out of his bedroom, smack into the twins. They giggled and stumbled.

'Finn! Careful!' declared Cordy, wagging a finger at her cousin. Finn gave them a pained smile.

'Sorry, girls.'

'Where're you going?' asked Cressida, spotting the backpack.

'Er, nowhere,' answered Finn quickly, hoping that her high, piping voice hadn't carried downstairs to Aunt C, who seemed to have bionic hearing.

'Just got to give your sister something.'

'What're you giving her?' asked Cordy, eyes bright with curiosity.

'Surprise,' said Finn, glancing at his watch.

Geoorgie suddenly came barrelling out of her room. She took in Finn and the twins, face tight with alarm.

'Finn. The Dark Meniscus is back!'

Finn turned to the twins. 'Love you girls. Bye.'

He grabbed Georgie, ran with her into her room, locked the door behind him and pushed the key out under the door so that Aunt C would be able to open it later without Johnny having to kick it down in a panic.

Finn grabbed Georgie's hand. 'Fred's bedroom. Are you ready?'

The twins were banging on the door, calling out. Georgie tried to block out the bangs, block out the growing desperation in their little voices.

She closed her eyes, concentrated with all her might.

'I'm ready,' she said.

Fred paced round his bedroom, hyperventilating.

'Hurry, please hurry,' he intoned, over and over again. He could hear the wind picking up, see the palm fronds begin their crazy dance.

The air around him shimmered and a second later, Finn and Georgie landed on his floor, none too gently. His mother called out from downstairs.

'Fred! Freddie! What's going on up there?'

They heard the clack of her heels on the marble stairs.

'Thank God,' said Fred. 'The Dark Meniscus - '

'I saw it,' said Georgie.

'Quick,' whispered Finn. 'Let's go.'

The three of them held hands.

'To the Castle of the Winds,' urged Finn. 'The courtyard. By the low table.' He said a silent prayer. Fred and Georgie's success at Astral Travel was patchy at best, and he knew that when his own powers were weak or over-used he sometimes failed too. Faith, he told himself.

Fred's mother's footsteps grew ever nearer. The roar of the wind grew ever stronger. Fred and Georgie screwed up their faces, *saw* with their minds. *Believe*, thought Finn, eyes desperate. Fred's mother grasped the door handle. Threw open the door. Upon an empty room.

CHAPTER FIFTY THREE

⌘ Hareb ⌘

THEY LANDED IN THE courtyard. They stood for a while, hands braced on knees, breathing, recovering. The birds playing in the fountain screeched with alarm and took to the skies, wheeling and diving in agitation.

The air rippled behind them. Shamal materialised, clad in a brown kandoora, a red and white checked shemargh bound round his head. He reached out to Finn, touched his arm. 'You made it.'

'Just,' exhaled Finn, his face halfway between a smile and a grimace. 'You too. Where's Hareb? Is he...' Finn couldn't say the words.

Shamal shook his head. 'He is not dead. He's alive, but he remains in a coma.'

'Where is he?' asked Fred.

'I'll take you to him.'

Hareb lay in a bed of soft white sheets. He didn't move, but his eyes were open. They stared straight ahead, fixed on some distant vision of hell.

'He knows, doesn't he?' whispered Georgie. 'He's conscious, awake inside himself. Trapped.'

Shamal nodded, eyes bleak.

Georgie took Hareb's hand, bent over him.

'Soon, Hareb. We promise you. We will free you.' She glanced up at the others. They came forward. Fred took Hareb's other hand. Shamal touched his arm, Finn touched his forehead. Fiercely they spoke the words, 'Soon. We promise you. Soon you will be free.'

CHAPTER FIFTY FOUR

❦ The Safe Room ❦

IN SILENCE, THEY RETURNED to the courtyard.
'You need to eat,' said Shamal. 'Regain your
strength.' He summoned Mrs Constance. A homely-
looking woman of about sixty waddled into sight bearing platters of food that she laid ceremoniously on the low
table. She cast sharp eyes at the four of them.

'Eat!' she commanded. 'Drink.'

'Mrs Constance, could you make up beds in the Safe
Room,' asked Shamal. 'My friends will be staying a while.'

'Will they now?' asked Mrs Constance with what looked
like the tiniest hint of a smile. 'Good. I'll do it right away.'

'So that's Mrs Constance,' mused Georgie, when the
woman had waddled out of sight.

'She might be highly evolved, but she looks like a scary
dinner lady,' said Fred.

'She's a LightFighter,' cautioned Shamal. 'I wouldn't
mess with her and I *would* eat her food.'

They nodded and complied, but they ate mechanically,
appetites shrunk by Hareb's plight and still traumatised by
all that had happened that day.

'Come,' said Shamal. 'Let me take you to the Safe
Room. You need to sleep now.'

Shamal lead them up a spiral staircase all the way to the top of one of the minarets. He paused before a door, shrouded by a billowing sand-coloured curtain. Shamal swept aside the curtain to reveal a door that seemed to be made of solid gold. He grasped the golden door knob and pulled open the door. He stood aside, gestured them in.

The walls were covered by more billowing curtains. Georgie took a peek behind one. Gold.

'Typhon cannot use his magnetic senses to track you when you are shielded by gold,' Shamal informed them. 'You should be safe anywhere in the Castle of the Winds, but, if Typhon were to come here, he would not be able to track you to this room, unless of course he followed you. Nowhere is completely safe, but this is as safe as it gets.'

Finn nodded. He surveyed the room; it was a large circular space with soft Persian carpets adorning the golden floors. Camel saddlebags, like rectangular, stuffed Persian rugs, were arrayed as seats around the room.

Mrs Constance had laid out thick duvets to lie on, more duvets to cover themselves, and a ton of soft-looking pillows to lay their extremely weary heads on.

Georgie almost whimpered with pleasure.

'Thanks, Shamal. This is great.' She had the feeling he was watching over them. His normally unlined face was creased with concern.

They pulled pyjamas from their backpacks, changed in the adjacent bathroom, then lay down on their beds. Shamal sat on one of the camel saddlebags, eyes full of questions.

Georgie too had her questions. 'Finn,' she said gently, eyeing the bruises on his head and the shock that dulled his eyes. 'What happened to you, back there on The Palm?'

'And what was with that thing you built around yourself in the classroom?' asked Fred. 'It was like a kind of force-field.'

Finn gave a weary smile. 'That's exactly what it was. Triton showed me how to build it. Just as well. It saved my life.'

Reluctantly, he told Georgie and Fred and Shamal what had happened.

'You killed the Policeman and his cronies. Well done,' said Shamal.

'They killed themselves, effectively,' replied Finn.

As he spoke, the adrenalin slowly left him. His whole body began to hurt like toothache, the pain warring with an overwhelming tiredness that flooded him. The Safe Room felt wonderfully cocooned. Finn just wanted to sleep, for hours, for days.

'Sorry, guys,' he mumbled. 'Just got to close my eyes for a minute.' The pillows were soft under his face, scented faintly of incense, and warm as if the golden floor and walls were somehow alive, possessed of their own heat. To sleep, to forget…..he tried to fight it. There were things he had to do. So many things….but then he was tired, so tired. He was drifting, drifting. Like falling off a cliff, he plummeted into a deep and dream-tossed sleep.

CHAPTER FIFTY FIVE

Postcard
from Cairo

SHOUTING, SHOUTING. WORDS PUMMELLING his head. Finn wearily opened his eyes. Fred was shouting at him.

'Finn! Wake up, mate.'

Finn snapped out of sleep and sat bolt upright, eyes raking round the room.

'What's up?' he asked quickly.

'I forgot!' yelled Fred. 'I meant to tell you last night but we all just fell asleep.'

'Wha - ' mumbled Georgie pushing herself up groggily.

'We need to find Shamal,' said Fred. 'C'mon. Quick.'

They found Shamal eating breakfast at the low table in the courtyard.

The Djinn boy stood, gave a courtly bow.

'Please, join me,' he said.

'We will, we will,' said Fred, grabbing a seat. 'But listen, I need to tell you something. Just when I was about to leave home last night I overheard my Dad yelling on the phone. Basically, Schmichael's been suspended. Dad was going on about some Museum reporting him for some wrongdoing.'

'Result Fred!' said Finn, grinning broadly. 'So your father keeps his job - '

'And,' cut in Fred, 'it's just possible that the Museum will move the Book of the Dead - '

'In which case, Mistral can track it,' finished Shamal with a look of admiration. 'Brilliant, Fred.'

Fred beamed. 'Well, hasn't happened yet, but…'

Shamal was already on his feet. He walked some way off, stopping close to the ever-burning brazier in which lumps of charcoal glowed and nuggets of incense burned. He stood motionless. Eyes closed, he breathed in the smoke. His face was creased with concentration. Georgie thought he seemed so tense he might start vibrating. After a minute or so, he began to sway very slightly and his lips moved in the faintest suggestion of a conversation. Suddenly the tension went out of his body and he seemed to sag. He took a moment, straightened himself, then walked back towards them, breathing deeply. Georgie could see the flush of effort on his face.

'We are in luck. I communicated with Mistral,' he said, smiling softly. 'She will contrive to tell Typhon that she has a feeling the Book of the Dead is on the move. That should make him let her out to see the stars tonight. Then, if the Book *is* on the move, she can track it. She can locate it for you.'

Fred got to his feet. 'I need to get the plans, familiarise myself with the lay of the land.'

Finn gave him a questioning look.

'*I* will get the Book of Dead,' declared Fred. 'I will Travel to Cairo, to the Museum. As soon as Mistral has tracked it, I shall go. I can read hieroglyphics, enough to recognise the Book, to be sure I have the correct book. And I know the layout of the Museum, well, from the drawings anyway,' he added with a modest shrug.

Georgie jumped up. 'I'll come with you. To help you.'

Finn got up too and opened his mouth to speak. Georgie intercepted him.

'No. You will stay here,' she said. 'You've been battered enough over the past few days. And you need to practise building your force-field, and, besides, if something happens to us in Cairo, then you have to be free to be able to go after the Burial Shroud.'

Finn grimaced. 'I'd much rather come with you. When and if Mistral locates the Book of the Dead, she will have to tell Typhon, won't she Shamal?'

The Djinn boy nodded.

'So you will be in a race with Typhon. What if he gets there at the same time as you do? I *want* to be there with you,' insisted Finn.

'To look after us. I know,' replied Georgie softly. 'But we'll be all right, Finn. We'll Astral Travel. We'll be in and out of that Museum faster than you can say *shark!* We'll be long gone before Typhon shows up. And, Finn, it's teamwork. Remember? We all do our bit.'

Finn didn't want to, but he could see Georgie's logic. He ran his hands through his hair, which still stuck up in all directions from his dream-tossed sleep.

'Better eat some breakfast then go and study those plans,' he said, forcing a smile. 'Shame,' he added. 'Always wanted to go to Cairo.'

'We'll send you a postcard,' replied Fred.

CHAPTER FIFTY SIX

Zephyr Trains
Finn

WHILE FRED AND GEORGIE pored over the plans of the Museum of Cairo and studied hieroglyphics, Finn paced the high battlements of the castle.

He looked out across the Rub al Khali at a view that would not have changed, save the shifting of the enormous dunes, for millennia.

Around him, the air quickened and shimmered. Finn circled round, bowed.

'Zephyr, my Lord, hello.' His eyes were grave. 'Thank you for saving my life.'

'Hello, my Prince. It was my pleasure. It is good to see you recovering. Now your strength returns and you are restless.'

Finn nodded. 'Fred and Georgie have their task, I want to get on with mine. I know what I *need* to do, that part's easy. I need to travel back in time, and through space, to the Valley of the Kings, to 1923 when Lord Carnarvon and Howard Carter opened the Burial Chamber and found the Burial Shroud. I need to intercept it, steal it and bring it back here.'

'That is your task. Yes.'

'But how on earth do I *do* it? I know *you* can travel through time, but how can *I*?'

'You ride the Winds of Time.'

A thrill ran through Finn.

'How?'

'I blow you along with me. You ride in my slipstream.'

'What's it like?' asked Finn.

'You know when you Astral Travel, when you travel through space you feel a force on your body?'

Finn nodded. 'You feel a great pulling, like you are passing through a tube. You feel squashed.'

'That is as nothing compared to travelling through time. You have heard of G force?'

'Gravity force,' replied Finn. 'Pilots of fighter jets feel it when they corner at speed. They need special training to withstand it. It can make you black out.'

'Correct. And the higher the G force, the greater the risk of losing consciousness. Of dying under the force,' added Zephyr.

Finn smiled. His new power should help him. He centred himself, he called up his power, felt the stirring in his blood, felt the heat emanating from him. He pushed out his force-field further and further in a flow of warmth and power and then he sealed it, seeing in his mind an impenetrable layer, clear as bullet-proof glass and just as strong.

'Will this protect me?' he asked Zephyr, turning in a slow circle, expanding his force-field, feeling it stretch away from his body. He knew Zephyr was near, but he could no longer feel him.

He heard a breath of wind.

'Hmmm. Very good. How strong is it, Finn?'

'I don't know. But it's saved my life already,' he answered, remembering the Policeman and the sink full of water.

He felt a punch, saw the air ripple and wrinkle before him, but nothing touched him.

'Very good. Ready for another try?' asked Zephyr.

Finn nodded. He heard the wind, then he was lying on his back, the air knocked from his lungs. He got up, eyes blazing.

'Do not be angry, Finn,' said Zephyr gently. 'You need to practise.'

Finn nodded. He got to his feet, built himself up, extended his force-field again.

'You know something of our enemy now,' continued Zephyr. 'You have encountered him several times. The last time you were all but killed. You will meet him again soon. You will offer him the trade, the Burial Shroud and the Book of the Dead for Mistral. And we will trap him. But he too will try to double cross us and you must be ready. This time, you must survive, conscious, alert, ready and able to fight. To train you, I must fight you myself. I will temper your force-field, harden it, so you will be protected. Are you ready?'

Finn took a deep breath, nodded.

'This will not be without pain,' warned Zephyr.

'I'm ready,' said Finn.

He stood waiting for Zephyr's onslaught. The wind slammed into him, knocking him back, pounding his force-field. Finn felt the blows, heard the raging of the wind in his ears. The Storm Djinn slammed into him repeatedly, hammering him.

Finn felt the burning as the friction of wind scythed across his force-field, but he kept it whole and unbreakable.

Sweat ran down his face and his body. He began to tremble and shake. His muscles and his mind screamed in protest, but he fought back. He fell to his knees and still the wind blew, knocking him flat onto his back. Finn fought to keep his force-field intact with all he had left. The wind picked him up, hurled him high over the battlements, held him there in its grip. Finn looked down, saw the rolling sand sea a quarter of a mile below. He felt Zephyr's power, but still he kept his force-field together. Finally, the wind relented, swept him back across the battlements, laid him down gently on the hot stone.

'You have done well,' intoned Zephyr. 'You are strong, boy Prince, stronger than I have ever seen you, stronger than any boy I have ever met across the millennia.'

Finn smiled. 'You didn't use all your power, though, did you? Not by a long way.'

'I used enough. I tempered your own power, made you harness it. You could never withstand a full-on assault by a Storm Djinn. You will need all your physical powers *and* your mental prowess to stand a chance against Typhon. What you did today will take you a long way. Enough for one day,' concluded Zephyr. 'We will resume tomorrow.'

Finn nodded. Relieved, he released his force-field.

'Now you must go to the courtyard,' said the Storm Djinn. 'See if my daughter communicates with her brother, if the Book of the Dead is on the move.'

CHAPTER FIFTY SEVEN

On the Trail of the Book of the Dead

THEY WAITED FOR THE stars to come out. First Venus, emerging in the darkening sky like a beacon. Then whole constellations shimmered in the gloaming. Here, above the Empty Quarter, the stars blazed down like a billion watching eyes. They waited, unspeaking, hoping, praying that Mistral would track the Book and communicate with Shamal.

Suddenly Shamal froze. He stood, listening, receiving, his body shimmering with energy. He nodded once, his lips moving silently. Then with a shiver, he broke from his trance and ran towards them.

'The Book of the Dead moved. Mistral tracked it. Give me your plans.' He studied them and pointed.

'There. That courtyard.'

'Courtyard?' questioned Georgie.

'It's in a van,' said Shamal quickly. 'They moved it into a van.'

'They're going to drive it somewhere,' said Fred.

'It's stationary now, or it was when Mistral and I broke off. If you go now, you should get to it. Go. *Quickly*,' urged Shamal.

Georgie shouldered her backpack. 'Ready Fred?'

He nodded, gripped her hand. 'Let's get in and out before Typhon appears. *See* the van. *See* the book. Let it draw us in, summon us to it.'

Geogie felt a fleeting panic about being summoned by a Book of the Dead. Fred began the countdown. 'Three, two, one…'

CHAPTER FIFTY EIGHT

∞ The Race ∞

FINN WATCHED THE EMPTY space where Georgie and Fred had been standing with a sense of deep foreboding. His gaze flickered up to the moon. A dark ring formed around it.

'The Dark Meniscus. Typhon's on his way,' he said grimly.

Shamal nodded. 'It's a race now.'

High above them Typhon powered through the atmosphere faster than a hurricane. In his mind he saw the van he had forced the captive Mistral to describe. It would be easy, he thought. He would suck up the van, smash it down again, peel it open like a can. The driver was dispensable. Any passers by on the street were dispensable. Nothing mattered save his goal. Then, in seconds, he would metamorphose into a man, grab the Book, secure it inside his suit, and walk calmly away with it, blowing any witnesses into oblivion. He would spin a tornado around him. He alone could walk through it, his Dark Matter weighing him down while all around him perished.

He smiled to himself. Cairo, how perfect! He even owned an apartment there, just minutes from the Museum. He would walk down the street with his prize, looking to all the world like the businessman he sometimes purported to be, out for an evening stroll. He would take the Book of the Dead to his apartment and he would read it. Cover to cover he would devour its secrets. The sixth Talisman, all its learning and all its power would be his. Then just one more Talisman and he would be invulnerable. Unbeatable. He would destroy the boy Prince of Atlantis who had evaded death time and again. He would obliterate and overturn the Travellers' cursed Prophecy. He would take on Zephyr himself, finally kill the Storm Djinn of the Light and steal his power to ride the Winds of Time. Armed with that, the whole world would be his. Past. Present. Future. He laughed. The thunderclap rolled through the heavens, down to hell.

CHAPTER FIFTY NINE

∽ The White Van ∽

GEORGIE AND FRED LANDED in darkness. They crouched, frozen like statues, holding their breath. Georgie reached into her backpack and fumbled for her Maglite. Her fingers found it. She clicked it on. They *were* in a van! She and Fred grinned at each other. Beside them was a large metal chest, strapped to the floor.

'Must be in there,' whispered Fred. He took a step towards it. A sudden thud resounded through the van as a door slammed, then, like an echo, a second door slammed shut. The van's engine kicked on with a throaty growl. Georgie and Fred braced themselves as the van lurched forward then turned violently, throwing them off balance. They slammed into the metal floor, stifling shouts of pain. They pushed themselves up and reached for the metal cage, desperate to find a handhold, when the van accelerated round another corner, throwing them over again.

'The driver's a maniac,' muttered Georgie under her breath. 'We've got what my mother would call a boy racer.'

'He's probably sixty,' said Fred. 'Let's hope we've got the right van,' he added. 'Anything could be in there.'

'Oh I think it's the right van. I can feel something, can't you?' asked Georgie.

'Like what?'

'Something Dark,' replied Georgie. 'Something evil.'

CHAPTER SIXTY

∽ The Silver Nile ∽

TYPHON COULD SEE THE lights of Cairo glittering below. The River Nile snaked through the
parched land like a slick of silver. It was turbulent
now, whipped up into a roiling fury. Typhon roared along
it, angling downwards.

He was down so low he could see the people gazing
up in fear as the wind buffeted their faces. Palm trees listed
crazily. People screamed as branches speared through the
air. Typhon laughed in wild delight. He saw the Museum,
huge and stately before him. He roared over, saw the courtyard. Empty. The van was gone.

His rage was blinding. It punched from him like an
explosion. It ripped the roof from a building, sent the metal
slicing through the air. He whirled round, searching feverishly, spinning the air into a tornado, sucking up cars, bicy-
cles, street lamps, people.

He flew off, dropping everything and everyone in his
wake. They fell to earth, never to fly again, never to see
again, casualties in a war they didn't even know was being
fought.

The van was white. Mistral had told him that. A
medium sized-white van. Typhon's eyes razed the streets.

He saw five white vans careering through the traffic. Which one? He calmed himself for a moment, tuned his senses, sought the evil he knew was waiting. The Spirit of Darkness had told him centuries ago. Find the Book, find the evil therein. He sought it, straining his senses, felt a pulse. There was another white van, weaving through the distant traffic a mile or so away. It came from there, he felt sure.

He raged above the city, aiming at it, eyes fixed on it, seeing nothing else. Gaining, gaining. The pulse of evil grew stronger. In seconds he would be upon it.

CHAPTER SIXTY ONE

∽ Caught! ∽

THE VAN SPED THROUGH the streets of Cairo, heading for the secure storage facility. The driver drove fast, hurrying to get the job done. He could see a storm approaching. Black clouds raced across the sky, blotting out the moon. He could see the palm trees bending under the onslaught of the wind as if they were flinching from blows. There was something in the air, a wildness. He somehow felt as if he were being *chased*.

Maybe it was the package, spooking him. The Museum Director, Mr Ismail, had avoided touching it, had made his assistant wrap it up while he stared at the package as if it were contaminated with some deadly virus. The assistant had then handed it to him and he had been forced to place it inside the metal box. Even through the muslin swathing it, he imagined he could feel something. Perhaps it *was* contaminated.

He shuddered. The sooner they delivered the package, the sooner he could get the heck away from it and out of this storm. He switched lanes, trying to gain a few yards, a few seconds.

Georgie and Fred stayed on all fours, flattening themselves on the floor as the manoeuvring of the van grew wilder still.

The van rocked violently. Georgie and Fred gasped as the van banked as if about to roll. With a great thud, it righted itself, flinging Georgie and Fred across to the other side.

'What was that?' asked Georgie, fear flickering in her eyes. Above the growl of the engines, they became aware of another sound. The screaming of the wind.

'Typhon!' they mouthed in horror.

Outside the storm seemed to be building. The scream of the wind grew louder, higher pitched. The van was vibrating. Suddenly, it lurched sideways, throwing them through the air again. They both crashed heavily into the side. They slipped down to the floor, groaning.

'God, the driver'll hear us crashing around,' said Georgie with a wince.

'Above this wind, maybe not. Let's hope not,' gulped Fred.

They braced themselves, waited for the next lurch, but the van slowed, cornered, headed downhill and stopped. The engine turned off. The screaming of the wind dropped. They could hear it, but the van no longer vibrated or shuddered in its grip.

'Let's see if the wretched Book is there and get the heck out of here,' said Georgie.

Fred rushed to the box, popped open the clasps, pushed up the lid. Georgie squinted over his shoulder. Inside lay a package, heavily swathed in muslin cloth. Saying a quick prayer, Fred lifted it out. As quickly as he dared, he unwrapped swathes of muslin, dropping them back into the box.

The last swathe of white cloth dropped away. In his hands Fred held a parchment bound book. The papyrus felt as delicate as a butterfly's wings. The hieroglyphics were faded, but still he could read them. He turned to Georgie, eyes shining.

'The Book of the Dead!' he declared.

'Time to get out of he – ' Georgie started to say. The words froze on her lips as the door to the van swung open. A short, powerfully-built guard with hard, dark eyes like bullets glowered at them. He blinked a few times, then like a gunslinger from the Wild West, he drew his pistol from his holster and pointed it at Fred.

CHAPTER SIXTY TWO

Bullet Eyes
and The Boxer

T HE MAN GLANCED FROM Georgie to Fred, then at the Book held in Fred's hands. He cocked his pistol and stepped closer. Another man appeared and started in shock when he saw Georgie and Fred. This one was very large. Scarily large. His fists, clenching by his sides, looked like boxing gloves and his nose, flattened against his face, looked like he had endured too many rounds in the boxing ring. The two men had a quick shouted conference in Arabic.

Fred tried to size up any possible escape routes. They seemed to be in some kind of huge underground garage, used for storage by the look of the boxes dotted around. Places to hide, maybe, if they could somehow get past the men.

'Who you? Why you in van?' asked the huge man in broken English.

'Er, well, it's sort of a long story,' started Fred.

The man glared at him, took out his mobile phone and tapped out a number. He spoke quickly, gesturing towards Georgie and Fred. Then he fell silent. He clicked off his phone and stared as if in a state of shock.

'Er, Sir, er what's going on?' asked Georgie.

The huge man, the Boxer, Georgie called him in her mind, threw his hands in the air. His face was red and sweat was staining his shirt.

'Goin on?' he demanded with a helpless shrug. 'Goin on? Whas goin on is two children in my van. Whas goin on is a hurricane in Cairo. All police, all services goin crazy. Palm trees flying through the air like missile. Police is busy. So, no Police to come arrest you for, for,' the Boxer faltered. 'How you get in my van? Was empty. Locked it myself.'

'You don't want to know,' replied Georgie. She glanced out of the back of the van, like Fred, trying to assess any possible escape routes.

She tried not to look at the short, stocky man, aware all the same that his cold eyes followed her every move with a look of hunger.

'So,' gestured the Boxer. 'Put down book, sit on floor. We wait until Police come.'

The stocky man, Georgie named him Bullet Eyes, seemed disappointed at this. He grunted, muttered under his breath. Fred reluctantly wrapped up the book and replaced it in the metal chest. The Boxer disappeared for a moment, then reappeared carrying two lengths of rope.

'Hands behind back,' he ordered.

'Wait,' said Georgie, mind racing. 'I just need a drink from my bag. It's hot, so hot in here.' She mopped the sweat from her face, allowing her arm to shake as she did so.

The Boxer nodded. 'Drink.'

Georgie fumbled in her backpack. Her fingers closed around the vial of sleeping potion. Quickly she found the water bottle and with deft fingers she tipped the sleeping potion into the water.

'Ah, water. Mr Violet's favourite potion,' said Georgie, eyes on Fred, praying he would get the message. She held the bottle to her lips, pretended to drink. Fred gave the slightest of nods. When Fred reached out for the bottle, Bullet Eyes greedily intercepted it and gulped down the doctored water.

Half left. He handed the bottle to the Boxer.

The Boxer took a good long drink then passed the bottle back to Georgie. There were just a few sips left.

The Boxer tied their hands.

The two guards sat on the floor. The Boxer periodically took out his mobile and dialled.

'Still hurricane,' he said, voice low with horror. They could hear it screaming overhead, even through the thick steel door which blocked their exit.

Bullet eyes said nothing, he just sat, eyes fixed on Georgie, his fleshy lips curled in a mockery of a smile.

Georgie wished she had her penknife on her. As a weapon it was pretty poor, but it was better than nothing. It was in her backpack, just two feet away, tucked into the side pocket, which was open. If she could just get it out, move it towards her.

She drew her knees up to her chin, blocking Bullet Eyes's view of her rucksack. She laid her head on her knees, pretending to sleep. Eyes open, she focused on her knife, she *saw* it in her mind. It was pink, three inches long, and her name was stencilled on the side. *Come to me,* she commanded silently, *come to me now*. She imagined she saw every molecule. She wriggled her curved fingers, summoning it. In her mind, she saw it sliding up and out of her backpack, sliding across the floor, up her arm and into her waiting fingers. *Believe, believe, see*. Something pink edged up out of the rucksack. Georgie nearly screamed in excitement. The penknife wobbled. It slid down the back-pack. Slowly it moved across the metal floor of the van, the slight scraping noise veiled by the screams of the wind which were growing louder again. Inches away, it was just inches away. Georgie wriggled her fingers. It slid into them as if it belonged there. She gripped it fiercely.

The steel door rattled and buckled. The screaming wind grew louder. Typhon must have tracked them, thought Georgie. He'd be through the door in seconds.

Fingers desperately struggling against their binds, Georgie flicked open the blade and began to saw it back and forth across the rope.

Bullet Eyes lurched to his feet and took a few groggy steps towards the van.

'You!' he shouted at Georgie. 'What you doing?'

Before Georgie could invent an answer, the lights died, plunging the garage into darkness.

CHAPTER SIXTY THREE

The Scissoring Door

THE LITTLE PENKNIFE SEVERED Georgie's bonds just as Bullet Eyes grabbed her arm. Georgie wheeled round, blade out and slashed at him. There was a roar of pain and rage and Bullet Eyes let go. Georgie swung back, tucked her legs against her then kicked out with all her strength. Her feet thudded into solid flesh and with another shout, Bullet Eyes tumbled out of the van and thudded to the ground.

Through the sound of blood roaring in her ears, Georgie could hear the Boxer shouting and floundering around. Georgie reached out for Fred. Her hands closed over an arm.

'Fred. That you?'

'Yes,' he whispered back.

'Hold still. I've got my knife. I'll cut the rope.'

She felt in the darkness for the rope binding Fred's hands. Quickly she cut through it. The roar of the wind grew louder.

'Now we need the Book,' hissed Fred through teeth clenched in fear.

A hand grabbed Georgie's ankle. She screamed and kicked out, but still the hand grabbed on. Georgie could hear movement on the floor as if the second guard were pulling himself up off the ground.

'Get the Book, Fred. Quick!'

She kicked out again, desperately this time, and the hand released her. She scooted back in the van, out of reach. She felt around for her backpack and found Fred's too.

Fred fumbled inside the metal box.

The roar of the wind grew louder and the steel door keeping it out began to groan.

'That door's going to blow in any second,' yelled Georgie.

'Nearly got it,' said Fred desperately. His fingers closed on the muslin wrapped Book.

'Got it!' he exclaimed.

Georgie reached for him in the darkness, found his arm, grabbed his hand.

'*See* the Safe Room. Let's go.'

Georgie heard a scuffling behind her and heavy breathing as one or both of the men tried again to get into the van. The potion had slowed them, but not stopped them. They were floundering, but not incapacitated.

Please, she thought. *See. Believe.*

There was a wrenching screech as the steel door ripped from its bindings. It scissored across the concrete floor, blown by the hurricane. By Typhon. Two tons of steel flew at the white van.

Leap…

Slicing it in two.

CHAPTER SIXTY FOUR

❧ The Fifth Talisman ❧

F INN PACED BACK AND forth in the Safe Room, eyes jerking to his watch every half minute. *Where are you?* He shouted into the empty air.

They should have been back ages ago. Half an hour had passed. He ran his hands through his hair, yanking at it in frustration and fear. He never should have let them go alone. Wild thoughts raced through his head. How would he ever forgive himself if -

'Aaaaaah!' Finn yelled as a body slammed into him, kicking him in the shins and knocking him to the floor.

'Georgie!' he shouted in delight. 'And Fred!' he called to the other tumbling body.

Fred and Georgie lay panting. Georgie rolled off Finn. 'Sorry about that,' she said with a grin.

'You're back!' said Finn, ignoring his throbbing shins. He grabbed Georgie and Fred and gave them a huge bear hug.

They grinned like maniacs, the three of them. 'Hey!' said Fred, raising his arm up. 'Careful. This thing is priceless.'

'You got it!' said Finn, voice awed.

Fred nodded. 'The Book of the Dead,' he said with a bow, unwrapping it and presenting it to Finn.

Finn took it gingerly. He held it in his hands, staring down at the faded parchment. Was it his imagination, or did it seem to pulse? A Talisman, thought Finn. It was easy to see why. He could feel the power in the Book just by holding it. *Read me, read me.* He heard the voice in his head. Was it his? He couldn't tell. The Book of the Dead. What secrets did it hold? Dark spells? Light incantations?

Finn put it down suddenly. His fingers tingled. He rubbed them roughly against his jeans, as if trying to remove a stain. He crossed the room rapidly and switched on all the lights, flooding the gloomy room with brightness.

His face paled when he saw what the gloom had veiled. 'Georgie, your tee shirt's got blood all down the front, and your arms are bloody, and your faces….. you've both got bruises everywhere. What the heck happened?'

'You're a fine one to talk. You've got a patchwork of bruises on *your* face. First I need food,' said Georgie. 'Food, loads of hot chocolate, then we'll tell you.'

'I second that,' said Fred.

Chapter Sixty Five

The Plan Accelerates

GEORGIE PEELED OFF HER bloody tee shirt and put on a clean one. She dropped the bloody one in the brazier, watched it burn. Shamal, pacing the battlements, waved down at them and ran for the staircase.

Zephyr cooled their faces, shimmering through the courtyard, susurrating the palm fronds.

'Well done Fred. Well done Georgie,' intoned the Djinn Lord as Fred held up the Book.

'Thank you,' they replied, bowing their heads in unison.

'You did it!' Shamal called, bursting from the staircase and sprinting across the courtyard.

'Brilliant! How d'you do it?'

'Just what I want to know,' said Finn. 'Have to wait for Georgie to refuel first.'

As if on cue, Mrs Constance arrived, bearing a tray laden with pots of hot chocolate and plates of muffins.

'Heard you clattering down the stairs,' she said. 'Thought you could do with this.'

Georgie smiled. 'Thanks. You're a mind reader.'

'Course I am,' declared Mrs Constance, before bustling off across the courtyard.

Georgie bit into a muffin. She washed it down with hot chocolate, then she and Fred began to speak.

'Thank God for Mr Violet and his sleeping potion,' Georgie said in conclusion. 'And for your penknife, Finn.'

Finn smiled. 'Never leave home without it. Pretty awesome, what you both did,' he added, eyes switching between Fred and Georgie.

'Thanks, mate,' said Fred. 'Glad to be back, I can tell you.'

'Me too,' said Georgie, suppressing a shudder.

'It is my turn now, my Lord,' said Finn. 'Typhon might come here, try to steal back the Book of the Dead and dole out some revenge for Fred and Georgie's beating him to it. I need to get the Burial Shroud and start to bargain with him, lay the trap.'

'Maybe you don't need to get the Burial Shroud,' said Georgie, eyes hopeful. 'Now that we have the Book of the Dead, maybe that's enough to bargain with.'

Finn shook his head. 'I don't think so. I think our only chance to manipulate him the way we want to is to offer him the two remaining Talismans. Then he would have the complete set. We have one chance at this, George,' Finn said emphatically. 'Remember with Hydrus and the pearl of Wisdom? We have to offer something so dazzling, something he wants so desperately that he won't be able to think straight. That way we get in under his defences.'

Georgie looked away. 'You're right,' she said dully. 'I just wish you didn't have to go.'

She looked back, studied Finn sharply. 'You want to go, don't you? You actually want to go!'

'To ride the Winds of Time?' asked Finn, voice full of wonder. 'You bet I do.'

Chapter Sixty Six

Thunder in your Soul, Lightning in your Veins

'YOU MUST PREPARE YOURSELF,' said Zephyr. 'You are right. Typhon will want to strike back at us. We must move before he does. Come. Follow me.'

Finn followed the Djinn Lord to the high battlements, an odd feeling of trepidation in his stomach.

Zephyr swirled around Finn. The air was warm, almost charged. Finn could feel it vibrating against his skin. The vibrations increased. His skin felt hot, then the pulsating air seemed to enter his body. He jolted, as if struck by invisible lightning. His whole body vibrated and it felt like electricity ran through his veins as the power surged from the Storm Djinn into him.

'Now you have lightning in your veins,' came Zephyr's voice. 'Now you have thunder in your soul. Now you have the power of a storm within you.'

Finn managed to nod. 'I can feel it. Thank you.'

Zephyr smiled. 'I am arming you, but the fight is yours.'

Finn could see the glow of golden eyes in the thickened air.

'So rest, Prince of Atlantis. You will need all your strength come morning.'

Finn could see Zephyr now, clearly, just for an instant. He appeared as a man, tall, brown-skinned, clad in a kandoora like Shamal, eyes huge and unreadable, but smiling. The man bowed low, then he was gone and the wind stirred restlessly again among the battlements.

CHAPTER SIXTY SEVEN

Death in all its Permutations

IN THE SAFE ROOM, after dinner, as the night deepened, Fred bent over the Book of the Dead, eyes frowning at the hieroglyphics. Every so often, he would scribble something down in his notebook before once again immersing himself in the body of the Book. Finn and Georgie slept, both of them muttering and twitching, trapped in dreams.

Fred consulted his dictionary of hieroglyphics. Yes, that was what it meant! He jotted down a translation, bent back hungrily over the Book. He read for hours, stopping for nothing. He felt a great presentiment of danger and some instinct told him that a solution to his unknown dread lay in the Book.

In his note pad, the chapter headings tumbled from his pen with the key notes gleaned from each:

How to hasten Death.

How to prolong Death.

How to Travel through Death into the Netherworld.

How to postpone Death.

How to reverse Death.

That one would be useful, he thought, chewing his pencil as he attempted to translate it. There were herbs, some he recognised, brewed into a tea. There was a vial of something he had never heard of which you poured into the mouth of the afflicted one. Bitter myrrh with darapaiso was as close as he could get in deciphering it. Handy that, he thought if ever any of them should come across it. And a chant, an invocation whilst the tea and myrrh thing was poured down the throat. Then the dead would arise, or so claimed the hieroglyphics.

Finally, Fred succumbed to exhaustion. The Book tumbled from his lap as he slouched into sleep. It closed with a snap, guarding its secrets from the night. But in his dreams, Fred read it still till the words ran into one stream ....death, death, death, death...

Chapter Sixty Eight

The Golden Whistle

THE MORNING DAWNED FIERCE and clear. Shamal handed a bundle of cloth to Finn. 'A jellabiya and a shemargh. Might help you blend in a bit with the Eqyptians.'

Finn went behind a pillar, stripped off his jeans and tee shirt and pulled on the jellabiya. He emerged and walked back to them. Shamal tied his shemargh and stood back to admire his handiwork.

'Very good. You're almost brown enough too. Apart from the green eyes, you'll do. And some Arabs have green eyes anyway.'

'Thank you,' said Finn, gesturing to his outfit. 'Must say, it's a lot more comfortable than jeans.'

'Just remember to hoik it up if you need to run,' said Shamal.

Finn nodded. He turned to Georgie and Fred, saw the love and the worry in their eyes.

'I'll be back as soon as I can. I *will* succeed,' he said, eyes fierce.

Georgie and Fred looked at him and they believed. Power shone from him. When he turned to walk away, his jellabiya fluttering in the breeze, he looked every inch the

Prince he was.

Zephyr blew around him. Finn felt the coiled, suppressed power of the Storm Djinn. And the goodness too. He felt it flowing into him.

'I have a gift for you,' Zephyr said.

Finn saw a flicker of gold. A chain hung suspended in the air. From it dangled a whistle.

'Take it.'

Finn looped the chain over his head, fingers on the whistle.

'It works. Try it,' urged Zephyr.

Finn blew the whistle. The finest note streamed from it like sunlight. Like magic. The air quickened around Finn as he blew.

'You may summon me with the whistle,' said Zephyr. 'Wherever you are. As long as we are in the same world, I will hear you.'

Finn felt a tremor run through him. The same world. If they became separated, in time, or kingdom, there would be no summoning. No help. *You fight alone,* said the voice in his head.

Zephyr's voice dropped to a grave rumble. 'Finn, before we go, there is something I must tell you. A warning. You will see sights to end all sights. You will see things that are almost irresistible. You will want to stop. You will want to linger. But there is no stopping. If you leap off the bands of time, you will be lost in time. If you see something that has meaning for you the temptation will be almost overwhelming. But you must resist it. You must! Do you understand?'

Finn wondered what might be so irresistible. An image came to him, then drifted out of reach. Something seemed to be calling to him but he could not quite hear it. He nodded soberly.

'Yes,' he said. 'I understand,' he replied, wondering if he really did.

'Good,' replied Zephyr. 'Live by that. Now, build your force-field.'

Finn shut out all else. He summoned his powers, drew the energy from his body, created his force-field.

The air started to vibrate. Muscular, grey-tinged clouds blew in. The rising sun looked febrile, glowing brightly as the clouds scudded across its face. There must be quite a wind up there, thought Finn, watching the clouds race.

The wind dropped down from the sky, spinning round him like a whirling dervish. Finn laughed out loud, half in terror, half in wild joy. As if in response, the weather grew madder. The sun glowed brighter, the wind blew harder, roaring through the battlements and across the Empty Quarter below. The water in the fountain erupted into a frenzy of boiling waves. Finn saw Georgie and Fred grab hold of each other, then flatten themselves against the courtyard.

Round and round swirled the wind, faster and faster. It hugged Finn, tightening around his force-field, roaring ever louder. And still the wind rose. Still the feverish sun burned until Finn felt as if the blood in his veins were bubbling. He felt as if he would evaporate or blow away, possibly both. He heard a voice, below the roaring of the wind, Zephyr's voice. *Ride*, it commanded, *Ride*...

Finn was airborne! He wanted to scream, to fight to stay moored to the ground. All his instincts told him he was going to die. But he did not scream. Instead he gave himself up to a wild exhilaration. He was flying, literally flying through the air.

CHAPTER SIXTY NINE

⤬ The Winds of Time ⤬

U P HE WENT, HIGHER than the battlements. He just had time to see Georgie's and Fred's faces, uplifted, open with wonder, before, like a missile, he shot off through the air. Finn felt the compression, but he had his own air to breathe, and he thanked goodness for it.

Far below him he saw the Empty Quarter stretching out like a huge, golden blanket over the earth. The Castle of the Winds was microscopic now. Up he went till the curve of the earth was visible below him.

Finn's eyes streamed as he rose higher still, gripped in the body of the roaring wind. He managed to get a hand forward, wipe his eyes. Then he saw colours, spinning round him in great loops. He had the sensation of slowing, of becoming suspended in the air. He could see now. Images, colours. Colours such as he had never seen before.

The longer he looked, the more he saw. Fields, great swathes of uncut forest, horses pulling carts, country lanes largely empty of cars, fields of men fighting. Spitfires dogfighting.

And he knew with a shudder of his heart what he was looking at. He was looking at Time.

He saw the loops of time spinning around the earth. They spun next to each other, year by year, millions of bands, the more distant from earth the further back in time. The colours were a new spectrum, one that had existed since the beginning of time, but one which no man or woman or child had seen. Until now.

He named them in his mind for the emotions they stirred in him; Courage, Birth, Love and Death, and more, so many more. He gazed at the colours, transfixed.

He saw pyramids in a desert, saw men swarming, tiny as ants. He closed his eyes. The compression grew stronger. He fought for breath. The colour of Death flickered unseen across his closed lids. Then he was gone.

Chapter Seventy

The Valley
of the Kings

S AND, WARM AND GRAINY underneath his cheek. A gentle wind on his face. Words. Distant voices. A close voice.

'Wake up now. You need to wake up. Finn, wake up!'

'Ergh!' Finn sat up abruptly, rubbing his eyes. Like a river running through his mind, it all came back. He scrabbled to his feet. Down a rugged hillside he saw the men, saw the site, the excavations.

He squatted back down on his heels, out of sight.

'We're here,' he whispered in awe. 'We're really here.'

'We are,' replied Zephyr, a smile in his voice. 'But now I must go. I will remain in this time, in this Kingdom, don't fear. But what you do now, you must do alone. I cannot break the Covenant. I cannot change history, so I must move away, out of the sphere of influence.'

Finn nodded. Gulped. Alone in another time. Alone in the past.

'You may summon me at any time with your golden whistle,' said Zephyr.

Finn nodded. 'I'll summon you as soon as I have the Burial Shroud. How long will it take you to come and blow us away, back to my time?'

'One minute.'

Finn processed this. Sixty seconds didn't sound long, but he knew from experience that if you were fleeing for your life each second felt like a minute. The difference between freedom and prison, life and death, could be measured in the fraction of a second. Had been.

'O.K. I'm going to crawl closer, scout them out. I don't think I'll make a move until night, but if I see my chance earlier, then I will.'

'I'll be waiting,' replied Zephyr.

Finn felt the Storm Djinn surround him, felt his warmth, felt the surge of his power. It flowed into his veins like euphoria, lingered there after the breeze had disappeared over the barren hills.

CHAPTER SEVENTY ONE

∞ 1923 ∞

F INN CRAWLED SLOWLY DOWN the rough hill. Loose
stones lay scattered like booby traps. A careless kick
and one could roll downhill, gathering momentum
and fellow stones, a noisy avalanche, shouting his presence
for all to hear.

Finn paused, wiped the sweat from his face with the
tail of his shemargh. It wasn't easy to crawl in a jellabiya. It
wouldn't be easy to run in one either. Better hope you don't
need to then, he told himself. But at least all this crawling
and sweat-wiping was good for his jellabiya. He had little chance of passing as a labourer in immaculately pressed
and clean clothes. He scrabbled amongst the rocks for some
loose soil, grabbed it and rubbed it over his face and hands
until he felt he looked suitably filthy.

He crawled on until he was perhaps three hundred
metres away from the outskirts of the camp. He found a
small outcrop, lay behind it, body screened, head poking
out, watching. He studied the scene below. Snaking col-
umns of jellabiya-clad men and boys carried baskets of rub-
ble and dirt aloft on their heads from a sunken pit to an
examination site a few hundred yards away. Here they lifted
out fragments, gently brushed the dirt from them and lined

them up in neat rows. Objects wrapped in swathes of white muslin were carried on stretchers by men with the slow careful gait of pallbearers. They were delivered into the many makeshift shelters which were dotted around. Some but not all the shelters were guarded. Finn studied these carefully. If the Burial Shroud had been found, it would most likely be in one of these shelters. But Finn reckoned there was a good chance it hadn't. It looked like the discovery of Tutankhamen's tomb had just been made. Most of the action seemed to be going on underground. If he were correct, the shroud was lying where it had lain for over three thousand years. Undiscovered, waiting. For him.

He froze as he saw an elegant, behatted figure emerge from underground. The man was wearing a three-piece suit, a bow tie and a pith helmet. He was closely followed by another man, similarly suited and bow-tied, also wearing a pith helmet. Finn's heart raced. Lord Carnarvon! And Howard Carter! Alive, both of them.

'1923!' he whispered to himself, still not quite fully believing what his own eyes saw.

The men spoke excitedly. Their posture was formal, like their suits, but excitement radiated from them. As well it might, thought Finn. Their last season digging in the Valley of the Kings. For six seasons they had dug, searched in vain for the fabled tomb of Tutankhamen. They had been on the verge of giving up, moving on. But, against the odds, they had believed. They had kept on going and they had succeeded. Finn felt an overwhelming admiration for the two men and a great sadness too.

He knew their fate. The Earl of Carnarvon had less than five months left to live. He would cut himself shaving in Cairo. The wound would fester, he would catch pneumonia and he would die, aged just 56. A victim of circumstance, or of the fabled Curse of the Mummy?

The men's voices drifted up the hill to Finn. He tuned in, picked up snatches of their conversation.

'We'll bring it out tomorrow...... into the store....... our tents. Double the guard.....attention....worried about things walking....got a feeling....'

Carnarvon suddenly looked up the hillside, almost as if he could sense Finn and his scrutiny. Finn resisted the urge to flatten himself. Like a hunting, or in this case, a hunted animal, he stayed still, tried to blend with the landscape. Carnarvon looked away, but Finn carried with him an impression of those eyes, glimpsed from a distance. Eyes that dreamed and eyes that saw. A Visionary's eyes, blessed now with the rare fortune of seeing his vision unfold before him.

CHAPTER SEVENTY TWO

∞ Infiltration ∞

FINN SETTLED IN TO wait for sunset. The sun beat down relentlessly on him. There was no shade on the barren hillside. His mouth and throat were dry and sore. He was desperate for water. He could see what looked like a food tent. Every hour or so the labourers would shuffle over to it, drink water and tea then resume their work. Perhaps he could risk it. He needed his strength. He was running on adrenalin, nothing more.

He leopard-crawled down the hillside, getting closer and closer to the food tent. Labourers came and went. Finn waited until he saw a large group of men and boys approaching the food tent. He crawled closer, then, as if dusting himself off, rose to his feet and dropped into line behind them.

He stood in a queue, trying to blend in, to be invisible. He used the trick Fred had taught him in the days when Fred was being bullied at school. Imagine you are grey. You don't exist. You are not here. It was hard, because every cell in his body felt radiantly alive, excited beyond belief.

As if conscious of that, the boy in front of Finn suddenly whirled round and stared at him, narrow-eyed. He asked a question in rapid, guttural Arabic. Finn coughed, affected a fit of coughing until he felt strong arms around him, words of concern, and a cup of water being pushed into his hands. He drained the water in one go, looked hungrily at the cup, glanced up at the man helping him. He was short and wiry, as if hard work and the rigours of life in the sun had burned every ounce of spare flesh from his bones. His wrinkled skin was brown as coffee, his nose was hooked like a hawk's and his eyes were bright and keenly intelligent. He produced a cup of tea, handed it to Finn. Finn sipped it. Heavily sugared. Heaven.

'Shokran,' Finn said, nodding. The man frowned slightly, ponderingly. He opened his mouth to speak, but a sudden manic pealing stole his words. A gong rang out, echoing against the steep valley walls. Finn watched a column of labourers file up and out of the earth, wiping sand and dust from their sweaty faces. They deposited their baskets and their rocky contents and hurried towards a collection of rough lean-tos. Finn watched them rummage through their scant belongings quickly extracting bowls and spoons. Then they hurried to the mess tent and joined the queue. Dinner time.

Finn glanced at the sun sloping down to meet the high hillsides. The end of the working day. He felt a nudge in the back. The hawk-nosed man, gesturing for his tea cup. Finn handed it back, was nudged along in the queue, closer to the cooks who were rapidly doling out small mountains of food. Finn shuffled ahead nervously wiping his palms against his jellabiya. Hawkman barked out a question to him. Finn shrugged. The man stared at him. His eyes were sharp like a hawk's too, thought Finn.

The fear of discovery beat in Finn's chest. *Stupid, stupid* to have risked joining the labourers. Finn fingered the cord round his neck, found his sea glass and fiddled with it. The man looked from the glass to Finn and back again. He reached out gnarled fingers, touched the glass, gazed at Finn in amazement. Finn stared back in amazement too. The glass had grown hot with the man's touch.

Hawkman turned abruptly and gave what sounded like a series of orders. Finn glanced around him rapidly assessing his escape routes.

Seconds later, a man appeared and handed Finn a bowl and a spoon. Finn blew out a breath. He bowed and said shokran both to him and to Hawkman.

Finn filed forward, proffered his bowl and saw it filled with rice and beans. He took a seat at a crowded table. Hawkman slipped in opposite him. He watched Finn eat from under heavily lidded eyes.

Who are you, wondered Finn, knowing only that the man had power. He wolfed down his food, nodded to Hawkman, returned the bowl and spoon to him. He rose to his feet, and, feeling the man's eyes boring into his back, he walked from the tent.

The sun had disappeared behind the valley walls and darkness was falling. Finn made his way towards the edge of the camp. He found an outcrop of rock, lay down hidden behind it waiting for the full cloak of darkness to fall on the land.

He gazed around, relishing the sudden stillness. There was the slightest of breezes. Was it Zephyr, he wondered, letting him know he was near? The breeze bore on it the rich tang of coffee, the very faintest whiff of incense. It carried with it snatches of conversation. Arabic. English. He peeked out from behind his rock. He saw the tall figures of the two Englishmen and a younger, shorter Englishwoman, Lady Evelyn, Carnarvon's daughter, Finn supposed. They were talking outside a row of four large tents fifty meters away. Living tents and storage tents, Finn reckoned. That would be the first place to check. If he did not find the Burial Shroud there, he would go into the tombs. He felt under his jellabiya. Strapped to his thigh were his Swiss army knife and his torch. He yawned, stomach full after his meal. He stretched out, gazing up at the darkening sky. Soon the stars would emerge. Five minutes, thought Finn. I'll just close my eyes for five minutes.

He plummeted into a sleep so deep he did not hear the footsteps, did not sense the man looking down upon him.

CHAPTER SEVENTY THREE

⚬ Dark Spells ⚬

THE CASTLE OF THE Winds was eerily quiet without Finn. Georgie and Fred sat in the Safe Room in anything but companionable silence.

'Fred, get your nose out of that Book,' said Georgie, elfin face taut with worry.

Fred looked up and for a moment his eyes were pools of blackness. Georgie shook her head, blinked furiously, and when she looked back at Fred his eyes were normal; blue, tired, concerned and just a tad irritated.

'Georgie, look, I can't explain it very well, but there's something in here. Something I need to know.' He frowned, rubbed at his left wrist.

Georgie looked down at the pale skin, at the faintest hint of red, of scar tissue not quite perfectly healed. Jehannem's burn, healed by her with Triton's sea glass, but perhaps the tiniest trace of Darkness lingered. That was Fred's fear. Hers too, for she and Finn both had been burned by Jehannem.

'There's evil in that Book, Fred. Darkness. I can feel it.'

'It's how it's used Georgie, not what's in it,' answered Fred, voice impassioned. 'There's life in it too. Healing.'

'And Death. Death everywhere. It's been used for evil. Can't you feel that?'

Fred put down the Book and studied his friend speculatively. 'It's a tool, Georgie. I can read it and I can use it. You don't understand it so you fear it. Simple.'

Georgie blew out a huge breath. 'Maybe you're right.'

Maybe she hadn't seen the blackness in his eyes. She was exhausted, waiting for Finn to return, distraught with worry, seeing things that simply weren't there, she told herself. She turned out her light, stretched out on the thick Persian rugs and sought sleep. But it brought no oblivion. Dreams stole in, and she saw clearly this time the Blackness in Fred's eyes.

CHAPTER SEVENTY FOUR

∽ Lord Carnarvon ∽

FINN AWOKE WITH A start. He pushed himself up, glancing round. He was being watched. All his Lightfighter's instincts screamed it. His eyes raked through the darkness but he could see no-one.

The moon rode high in the sky, brilliant against the blackness. How long had he slept? How *could* he have let himself go like that? He stayed still and listened. A distant cough. The faint echo of a dog's bark.

The camp was asleep. Time to move. Finn got down on his stomach and slunk towards the tents where he had seen Howard Carter, Lord Carnarvon and Lady Evelyn talking. He crawled on, skin prickling with danger, unable to shake the feeling of being watched.

The night was hot. The air clung to him, humid, stagnant, unstirred by any breeze. Where was Zephyr? A minute away, Finn told himself. He checked the golden whistle was still round his neck. It was. He pulled it out from under his jellabiya. Ready, just in case.

The tents were twenty feet away. So was a watchman, asleep in a chair, rifle lying on the ground by his side. Finn watched him for a while, seeing his chest rise and fall. He crawled closer. Ten feet away. Crawling was too noisy. His jellabiya made a soft scraping sound against the ground. Noiselessly, Finn straightened up. On bare feet, he tiptoed across the beaten sand towards the open mouth of the tent.

He passed the sleeping guard, so close he could have touched him. He stepped into the tent, took a few paces in, stepped to the side so that he would be unseen by anyone who chanced to be passing. His heart was slamming against his ribs now. He fought to keep his breathing calm.

His eyes adjusted quickly to the gloom. The light of the moon scarcely penetrated here, but Finn could not risk his torch. He saw the glint of gold everywhere; animals, statues, boxes, a tray glittering with jewelled knives, a huge, long sarcophagus. Finn gasped. The golden coffin of Tutankhamen! Dare he touch it? Would he be cursed if he did?

He reached out towards it and screamed as a hand grabbed his arm in a vice-like grip. He wheeled round, struggling.

A tall, elegantly pyjamaed man with a thin moustache glowered at him.

'Lord Carnarvon!' gasped Finn.

The guard, alerted by Finn's scream, floundered in.

Carnarvon spoke to him crisply. 'Light the lamp Magdi, then wait outside. Awake this time.'

The guard lit the lamp, then shooting Finn a look of fury, he left the tent and took up position outside.

Lord Carnarvon turned back to Finn. 'Who the devil are you?'

'If you'd let go of my arm, I'll tell you.'

Carnarvon barked out a laugh. 'You are bargaining with me?'

'No. I'm just asking you to let go. You're bruising my arm.'

Carnarvon let go. 'Well, we can't have that, can we? A

thief breaks into my tent and I bruise his arm.'

'I'm not a thief,' said Finn. That wasn't strictly true, he thought. He was intending to be one, once he found what he was looking for.

'You are a well-spoken English boy with nerves of steel, disguised as a local. Caught poking around in my tent. Why?'

Finn glanced around. This was getting complicated.

'No, I wouldn't try to escape,' observed Carnarvon drily. 'The guard, Magdi, has been profoundly humiliated by being found asleep on the job. He is simply itching to make up for it. He'd shoot you down like a cur.'

He would too, thought Finn. He took a deep breath.

'Look. It's a long story.' He rubbed his face. 'I can't believe I'm talking to you.' His mind raced. He needed to get out of here, but he had no intention of going back to the Castle of the Winds empty handed. Taking advantage of the light, he looked around. Gold. Solid gold. A mesh, a golden mesh. He contrived to turn. A body-sized mesh. The Burial Shroud! It had to be! Locked away inside a glass case. Finn quickly veiled the excitement in his eyes. He looked back at Lord Carnarvon.

'I've got a message for you,' he said determinedly. 'Look after yourself. Don't shave.'

Carnarvon's mouth twisted wryly. *'Don't shave?'*

'Yes. Grow a beard.'

Carnarvon watched Finn with a look of amusement tinged with disbelief.

Finn took his chance. He'd have to come back here later, but for now, he had to escape. He'd seen the pictures. He *saw* the Burial Chamber in his mind. He imagined it. Cool, slightly fetid, still. Dark as night. *See. Believe. Leap*. He heard Lord Carnarvon's distant exclamation as he vanished.

CHAPTER SEVENTY FIVE

The Spirit
of Darkness

OLD AS DEATH. SILENT as the grave. Finn stood still. He *was* in a grave, he felt sure of it. He reached under his jellabiya, unstrapped the torch, keeping a firm hold on it. He prayed it would work. He didn't like small, enclosed spaces very much, especially not in pitch darkness, a darkness deeper than any he had ever seen. Heart racing, he flicked the switch.

A plume of light shone out, lit up ochre walls painted with images of gods and goddesses, hieroglyphics, symbols, ghostly figures clad in white, and, over and over again, the image of a young man, slender, beautiful, royally adorned. There was an empty space, delineated by marks on the stone floor, where the burial casket would have stood. Tutankhamen's Burial Chamber! Finn sank to the ground, sat cross-legged, eyes wide with awe. The hieroglyphics were spells from the Book of the Dead, he remembered that from a lesson at school. What did they say, he wondered, these spells?

There was no Burial Shroud. The contents of the room had been removed. All that was left were the spells on the ochre walls and the images, vivid and haunting. A black hole gaped where the entry had been made into the Burial Chamber. Beyond it lay the shadows of another room.

Finn paced round, studying the spells. He noticed a small cleft in the wall and in it a tiny shelf. On the shelf stood a small, dark blue bottle, imprinted with faint hieroglyphics. Acting on instinct, Finn grabbed the bottle, shoved it into his pocket.

He heard a faint sound, a whooshing rasping, like a sword being drawn. He wheeled round but there was nothing, just him and the empty room and the spells. It must have been his jellabiya, he reasoned, rasping against the ochre walls.

Either way, he wanted to leave now, to get out, to *travel* back to the area behind Lord Carnarvon's tent, but he dared not do it too soon. He couldn't risk another encounter with the man, especially not after he'd been seen disappearing into thin air. He'd best give it a couple of hours, in which case he'd better conserve his batteries. He took a deep breath and turned off the torch.

Darkness flowed back into the chamber like a river. It engulfed him. It was so dense, so complete, it seemed to Finn that he could feel its weight pressing down on him. He shuddered. It felt almost alive. Carefully, he strapped his torch back to his thigh. He sat, cross-legged breathing the dank air. Was the tomb sealed overnight, he wondered? How much air was trapped inside? Would it run out? Would he even know it as slowly, slowly, the oxygen failed and he fell into what he thought was sleep. Eternal sleep.

He stood abruptly. He felt something. The faintest stir in the darkness. All his senses screamed, ready to fight an unseen enemy. He stood, waiting, but there was nothing.

You're imagining things, he told himself sternly. *Spooked by the dark. Don't panic,* he chastised himself. *You'll only use up more oxygen if you do.*

He sank down to the cold stone again, crossed his legs. He thought of Tutankhamen, mummified, lying here in his Burial Chamber for over three thousand years. What would it have been like to be the boy king, the Pharoah? Tutankhamen had died, perhaps been poisoned, just as he was entering manhood. Finn felt as if the echoes of those times were still playing through the tomb, just below the level of human hearing. He had the strangest sense that the walls were whispering ancient secrets, mysteries taken to the grave, waiting for millennia to be released.

Who killed you, Tutankhamen, he whispered? *Who did it?*

Enemies. Trickery. The boy had enemies. The words slid through the darkness.

Finn started in horror. He jumped to his feet, reached for his torch, fumbled, heard the clatter as it fell and rolled away.

Gone, said the darkness.

Finn stood absolutely still, not breathing. Only his eyes moved, raking through the blackness, seeking the speaker.

Eyes will not see me.

'Who are you? asked Finn, a tremor in his voice.

I am the Spirit of Darkness. I see the hidden in men's souls. I see the evil.

Finn wanted to see, desperately wanted to see. He calmed his breathing, summoned his powers, tried to project the Light from him. Seconds passed. The darkness remained absolute. No Light came from him. He felt a surge of panic, crushed it quickly, redoubled his efforts. Nothing happened. Now he felt real fear. Here, inside the Burial Chamber, in the presence of this Spirit, he could not use his power.

There will be no light here.

It was a statement of fact. And a threat. Whatever the heck was in the Burial Chamber with him, it had enormous power.

'What do you see?' asked Finn.

I see the enemies, hiding as friends. The boy Prince had them. The boy Prince has them.

'Which Boy Prince?'

A rippled passed through the darkness. It felt like laughter.

Why, you of course.

'Who?' asked Finn, mind racing. 'Who are my enemies?'

Close. Sacrifice. You do not See.

Finn heard a sound. A thud. He was sure of it.

'Who?' he demanded.

Footsteps approached, the faintest flicker of light.

Do not trust. Do not trust.

The Darkness retreated abruptly. It seemed to enter the walls, but before it had departed completely, it spoke again, its voice suddenly shrill.

Payment. I will have Payment.

Finn quailed. It spoke the words as a kind of dark promise. As a curse.

An arm thrust into the room, bearing a flaming torch. Hawkman!

CHAPTER SEVENTY SIX

☙ The Traveller ❧

'E R,' MUMBLED FINN, BOTH delighted to see the man and dismayed at being caught.

Hawkman glanced nervously around the room, seeking. He made an abrupt gesture with his hand, indicating that Finn should follow him.

He stepped outside the Chamber, taking the light with him. As he did so, Finn felt the Darkness flow again from the walls.

Hawkman hurried away, as if he had some inkling of what waited in the Burial Chamber. Finn rushed after him, staying close as he wound his way through passageways and chambers with the authority of one who knew them blindfold.

Finn glimpsed gold; ankhs, fans, running dogs, cats and urns and more frescoes depicting pharaohs triumphant in battle.

They turned another corner. Hawkman paused before a flight of stairs. He raised his finger to his lips in the universal gesture of silence. Slowly, he tiptoed up the steps, paused at the top, waited. Finn was desperate to get out, but he waited, heart hammering. At last, Hawkman beckoned. Finn mounted the steps, walked out into the night, gulping in air. He felt a sudden wave of sickness roll through him. He fought it down.

Hawkman beckoned again. Finn glanced around. He could follow him. He could run away, but this man had fed him and he had saved him. Finn owed him a debt. That and curiosity made him follow.

They walked past another sleeping guard, past rows of sleeping labourers. They went beyond the boundaries of the camp. The moon was sinking in the sky. Soon it would be dawn.

Hawkman picked a spot beside some boulders and sat cross-legged. Like a viper striking, he grabbed Finn's arm, pulled up his sleeve exposing his upper arm. Finn pushed him off with a snarl, grabbed Hawkman's jellabiya and repeated the gesture. Finn's eyes widened as he saw what Hawkman had sought on his own arm; an inoculation mark, the rough circle of a TB jab. They didn't exist in 1923.

'Who are you?' Finn asked, heart racing in shock.

Hawkman gave an enigmatic smile.

'I am a Traveller,' he answered, in perfect, lightly-accented English.

'I go back and forth, seeking,' he added.

'How? How do you go back and forth?'

'I ride the Winds of Time. When they blow. If I am near I can feel them.'

'And you work as a labourer on an excavation?'

'Foreman. And it's not just any excavation, is it?'

'No, it's not. What are you searching for?'

'The Prince who walks through Time.' Hawkman, the Traveller, smiled.

'I felt your power as soon as I saw you. The Spirit knew

who you were at once. He sees the hidden in men's souls, but I would have suspected you anyway. We have been waiting a long time for you.'

'Who's we?' asked Finn, mouth dry with fear.

The Traveller took a whistle from under his jellabiya. It was jet black. He blew.

'Why, Typhon, of course. And today I shall deliver him the Burial Shroud. And you!'

'So you helped me, only to betray me,' said Finn, thinking of the Spirit of Darkness and its words of warning.

Hawkman shrugged. 'We Travellers spin and twist. We pick up the colours of time. We collect Light and Dark. I am tinted, tainted, call me what you will, imbued by the Darkness that surrounds me. I have no Will. So I cannot betray.'

'You just did,' yelled Finn, leaping to his feet.

'There is no escape,' shouted the Traveller as Finn ran towards the tents. 'Nowhere to hide.'

CHAPTER SEVENTY SEVEN

Death Mantle

FINN SPRINTED TOWARDS LORD Carnarvon's tent. His feet felt heavy. His body felt as if it were under some kind of attack. The wave of sickness hit him again and he felt horribly ill. He slowed just outside the tent, blowing hard. The guard was nowhere to be seen. Finn heard a sound, running water, peeked round the tent and saw the guard urinating. He ducked back round and hurried into the tent. Saw the Burial Shroud, laid out in a glass case. With a padlock.

He took out his own whistle and blew as hard as his straining lungs would allow. He blew and he prayed. Then, heedless of the noise he would make, he picked up a paperweight and smashed it into the glass. He knocked the shards away with his elbow, carefully removed the Burial Shroud. He laid it over his arm, whirled round to see Lord Carnarvon standing five feet away, levelling a pistol on him.

'You!' expostulated Carnarvon. 'I wondered if you would return. Who are you? And how the devil did you just disappear? Are you a God, a Demon? What *are* you?'

'You want the truth?' asked Finn.

'Course I want the truth.'

'I am a Prince of Atlantis. I have travelled back in time to take this Burial Shroud. I take it not for myself, but to prevent a great evil. I am fighting a battle. I am fighting a war. A war of the Djinns. And I need this….' Finn felt a wave of dizziness assail him. He struggled to focus. He shook his head, drew on his strength. 'There's no time. I must go. Now. With this. Trust me. Trust me and let me go.'

Carnarvon studied him, eyes boring into his like lasers. 'I'd always believed,' he said, voice soft with awe, 'that other things existed, beyond what we can see. Now I meet you. I believe you. Go.'

Finn reached out, shook his hand.

'Thank you! Thank you!' he said, fervently. 'Now, hide. Get under ground. There's going to be a terrible shamal. In minutes.' He spun on his heel and ran from the tent.

Hawkman stood there, face a mask of patience as if he knew there was nothing Finn could do to escape.

Dawn was breaking, the sun had risen above the harsh stone mountains. Finn could see the dark meniscus, sinister against the pink of sunrise. Typhon was on his way. But so was Zephyr. Finn could feel him coming. He felt the shudder in the air, felt the breeze grow, then suddenly, Zephyr was upon them, swirling around them.

Zephyr hissed.

'Finn, what has happened? You are mantled with Darkness.'

Finn felt his stomach roil in fear at the tone of Zephyr's voice as much as at his words.

'It is a Death Mantle. I must blow it off you. Now. Stand. Root yourself to the ground. Do not move.'

Hawkman watched, impassive, as Zephyr spoke, as the wind swirled around Finn.

Finn felt it suck at him as the sickness inside him seemed to multiply. The wind scoured his skin. Sand penetrated his mouth, his ears, his eyes. The sickness burned within him, warring with the wind. He felt like screaming as Zephyr tore at him, raged around him. Finally he felt the sickness abate and with it the wind.

'Has it gone? Has it gone?' Finn asked desperately.

'It has gone,' came back Zephyr's voice. There were still traces, the Djinn could see them, but there was no time to remove them.

Finn froze. He heard the wind picking up, the low growl of thunder in the air. Typhon.

The Traveller smiled. 'My Master comes.'

Zephyr stilled. Finn felt his power coiling. 'Where do you come from, Traveller?'

Finn saw Lord Carnarvon standing outside his tent, watching, listening, eyes wide with wonder. Finn closed his eyes, focused in. He summoned up his powers, built his force-field. He projected it, strengthened it, ignoring Carnarvon, ignoring the howl of the wind, ignoring all but the need to complete what he had started.

'Let's go,' urged Zephyr.

Finn opened his eyes. 'He hitches a ride on the Winds of Time,' he shouted, pointing to the Traveller. 'He'll try to come with us.'

He called out to Lord Carnarvon. 'Please, Sir, can you keep him away from us?'

Carnarvon eyed the man, walked towards him, face grim. 'Get over there,' he gestured with his pistol.

'Get him underground,' pleaded Finn.

Carnarvon thought about this for a moment, then nodded. He angled the gun at the Traveller. 'Go,' he commanded.

'And don't shave,' yelled Finn. 'Don't cut yourself.' His words were blown away as the forerunners of Typhon slammed into them.

'Are you ready?' asked Zephyr. Finn felt his force-field. It felt ragged, incomplete. But Typhon was almost upon them. He felt Zephyr swirl around him, felt the power of the wind grow. Then he was airborne, caught in the tumult as Typhon hit Zephyr. He felt the battle, he heard the screams of the winds as the Storm Djinns fought. Wind slammed into wind, with him in the middle. *Keep the force-field*, he urged himself. *Keep the force-field*. But he was weak. Weak from the Death Mantle, from the damage it had done before Zephyr blew it off him, weak from his first voyage on the Winds of Time. His eyes blurred as blood vessels burst. He felt the blood, warm on his skin. His force-field was taking a pounding, weakening, weakening. He felt himself failing. He tried to fight. With all his being, with all his powers, he tried to fight. Until he could fight no more and Darkness closed in.

CHAPTER SEVENTY EIGHT

Death and the Spell

GEORGIE AND FRED STARED at their breakfast. Neither of them could touch a thing. Finn should have returned ages ago. They watched Shamal pacing around the courtyard. His kandoora hung limply on him. There was no breeze with Zephyr gone. It felt like there was no air.

Georgie glanced up. High in the sky, she saw the clouds racing.

'Fred. Look!'

Fred raised his head, saw the tumult above. Then, in seconds, the wind hit them. It scorched across the courtyard, screaming its fury, then it rose up.

'The Safe Room,' yelled Georgie. She and Fred set off at a sprint. A blur shot past them. Shamal! They raced up the spiral stairs, found Shamal battering the closed door.

'Father, please, let me in.'

The door flew open and they all rushed in. Finn lay prone, a garment of spun gold wrapped round his arm, clenched tight in his fist.

Georgie and Fred fell to their knees beside him. Georgie took his face in her hands while Fred felt for a pulse.

'What happened?' shouted Georgie, voice desperate.

'Finn went into the tomb,' said Zephyr heavily. 'He came out with a Death Mantle over him. I blew it off, but it weakened him. Then Typhon came. There was a battle. Finn's force-field wasn't strong enough. I'm sorry.'

'Noooooo,' screamed Georgie. Finn could not be dead. It was not possible.

'There's no pulse,' said Fred, voice hollow. He stared straight ahead, eyes looking in, face a mask of concentration.

'We have to try it. A reversal spell from the Book of the Dead. Georgie,' Fred said sharply. 'Do exactly as I say.'

Georgie nodded, eyes streaming with silent tears, her heart and mind in revolt at what she saw before her.

'Hold Finn's hands in yours, grip his wrists. Repeat the words I say. You won't know them, just repeat them.'

Fred jumped up, got the Book of the Dead, paged through it frantically until he found what he sought. He hurried to Finn's side, removed the golden shroud from his arm. As he did so, a dark blue bottle rolled out of Finn's pocket. Fred grabbed it, studied the hieroglyphics, eyes widening.

'It's the restoration elixir the Book speaks of. He must have found it in the tomb.' Fred's eyes gleamed with hope. He grabbed Georgie and shook her shoulder. 'We have a chance now, George. We really do. Believe. Please believe.'

She looked into his eyes, saw the belief there, tried to shut out the image of Finn's body, dead by her side. 'I believe,' she said, voice hoarse.

Fred unstoppered the ancient bottle. A voice in his head said, *what if it's poison? What if it kills him?* You can only die once, Fred answered himself, then shut off debate. He glanced at the Book, tipped up the bottle, watched a drop fall slowly. It was dark blue, thick. It fell between Finn's open lips. Fred tipped out another two drops. Then he took Finn's head in his hands and incanted the words of the Book of the Dead.

He wasn't sure how they should be pronounced, he just said them as he could:

'Lentementad, archisteez, gspaaqqemed, argngoos.'

He repeated them three times, just as the Book ordered. Then he released Finn's head, closed the Book and watched.

Georgie let go of Finn's hands. She moved them instead over his body.

'Call on your own powers, Fred, call on your light, flood Finn with it.'

Together, Fred and Georgie moved their hands through the air above Finn's body, summoning their powers. Every last molecule of power they drew up, they sent out to their friend.

'Please, Finn,' said Georgie, after minutes had passed. 'Please, wake up.'

The tears raced down her cheeks, and down Fred's.

'No, Finn, please, come back, come back,' begged Georgie. Her tears fell upon his face, wet his cheeks, wet his lips, flowed onto his eyelids.

It was unthinkable that Finn, their friend, who had been through so much, who had survived so much, could be dead. But their eyes could no longer deny what they saw. Finn lay unmoving, unbreathing. Still and dead.

Chapter Seventy Nine

⟳ Reversal ⟳

GEORGIE REACHED OUT A hand, wiped her own tears from Finn's face, froze.

An eyelid moved. She was sure of it. She bent closer, stroking his face.

'Finn,' she whispered, 'Finn, keep travelling. Back to us. Back to us, Finn.'

The eyelid flickered again. Both eyelids flickered. Georgie kept her eyes on Finn.

'Did you see that, Fred?' she gasped. 'His eyelids moved.'

Fred kneeled beside her.

'George. It's too late. It's – ah. Fiiiiiiiiin!' yelled Fred.

Finn lay below them, eyes open. For a moment, his eyes stared straight ahead, his gaze on some faraway place, then slowly, his focus came back, to the room, to them.

'Hi,' he croaked. Georgie and Fred fell upon him in a bear hug. With what strength he had, which wasn't much, Finn hugged them back. They lay for minutes, hugging, laughing, weeping together, then Georgie gathered herself.

'Right, you need food. You need water.'

She turned to Shamal, to ask for some, but Shamal, Zephyr and the Burial Shroud were all gone.

CHAPTER EIGHTY

Who are the Enemies?

G EORGIE FOUND SHAMAL IN his room. He had hung up the Burial Shroud and was gazing at it. Georgie felt fury flood through her.

'Stop staring at that thing.'

Shamal whirled round, eyes wary.

'He's alive!' she shouted. 'Finn's alive.'

Shamal bowed his head in a gesture that seemed to Georgie to be half relief, half shame.

'Alhamdullilah. A miracle.'

'Yes, a miracle,' replied Georgie. 'Now he needs food. Broth, dates, water. In the Safe Room. Please.'

Shamal nodded. He walked from his room, casting a quick look over his shoulder at the Burial Shroud.

Finn sat up against a small mountain of cushions. He sipped sparingly from the bowl of broth that Georgie held to his lips. Slowly, the colour returned to his skin. He ate three dates, drank two cups of water, then he told Georgie and Fred everything that had happened.

'Finn, this Spirit, you said it warned you. What exactly did it say?' asked Georgie.

Finn did not want to go back into the Burial Chamber. Never wanted to hear that voice again, but he forced himself to remember.

'*I see the enemies, hiding as friends*', it said. '*The boy Prince had them. The boy Prince has them.*'

Finn shuddered. 'I asked it who were my enemies? It didn't say, just said:

'*Close. Sacrifice. You do not See. Do not trust. Do not trust.*'

Finn rubbed his hands over his face, banishing the memory. 'That's all I know.'

Fred thought for a while. 'D'you think it meant Hawk-man, the Traveller?'

Finn stared into space. 'It could have done. He was close. He did betray me. But the Spirit said enemies, plural, and spoke of sacrifice.'

Finn yawned massively. 'Sleep. Need to sleep.'

He sank down. Georgie pulled his duvet over him, tucked it under his chin.

'We'll watch over you. Sleep well.'

Finn smiled and plummeted into sleep.

Georgie looked across at Fred. His eyes, like hers, were deeply troubled.

'Are you thinking what I'm thinking?' she asked, 'about the enemy?'

He nodded. 'I'm afraid so.'

CHAPTER EIGHTY ONE

Normal for
One Day

F INN SLEPT THROUGH THE rest of the day and the whole night, waking at dawn the next morning. He got up, paced around the Safe Room. He still felt weak, weak and sick.

Fred and Georgie sat up, awakened by Finn's pacing.

'You all right?' asked Georgie worriedly.

Finn shook his head. 'Still feel a bit off. Look, guys, I know this won't be popular, but I want to go back, just for the day. I need to see Triton.'

To Finn's amazement, Georgie nodded. She could see Finn wasn't back to normal. His eyes were haunted still, shadowed with a darkness that she knew was death.

'Go,' she said. Perhaps Triton and the sea would banish those shadows.

'Go now,' said Fred, glancing around. 'Don't tell anybody, just go.'

Finn eyed Fred. 'Why all the secrecy?'

'No secrecy, just simpler, isn't it, not to tell Shamal or Zephyr, deal with all the fuss.'

Finn knew what they weren't saying. He was trying not to think it too. Shamal could be his enemy, even, remote possibility as it seemed, so could Zephyr. A look of strange weariness passed over Finn's face. For now, he didn't want to suspect the Storm Djinn of the Light, or his son, who had after all saved them once. He just wanted to get out of here, get back to the sea, to his own element.

'Be careful, Finn,' said Georgie. 'Be back before sunset, please.'

He hugged her and Fred. 'I will.'

He moved away, closed his eyes and focused on Shell Beach. There was a small section, round by the fishermen's village, beyond the walkers' route. You had to pass through the sea to get there, it was sheltered, hidden. Unless of course some intrepid walker had just happened to go there. In which case, thought Finn, he or she was going to get one heck of a surprise.

See. Believe. Leap. Finn disappeared, watched by unseen eyes.

Chapter Eighty Two

❦ Shell Beach ❦

FINN LANDED, CATLIKE, ON all fours on the hidden beach. He saw with relief that it was empty, save for a black cormorant. The startled bird eyed Finn with outright hostility. Finn knew these birds. They could be seriously aggressive and it looked as if the bird was considering an attack. Finn laughed.

'Have pity,' he called. He took his eyes from the bird, clocked the sea with a whoop of joy. Waves, big ones, rolling in like thunder.

He ran into the water, evading the flapping black wings and the beak aimed at his shoulder, laughing, diving under the crashing waves. He swam out back beyond them, before they broke. There he lay on his back, rising and falling with the swells as they powered under him, rocked by the sea, revelling in being alive. The sky above was a perfect blue, the sun was hot, the water warm. Tears streamed down his cheeks, tears of joy, tears of relief, and unshed tears of horror. Like absolution, the sea washed them away with tears of its own.

He felt his strength coming back to him. He swam with the waves, surfed with his body as they broke, let them carry him like an arrow to the beach, mantled in foaming water. Again and again he swam back, caught the waves. Only when he was feeling thirsty did he reluctantly drag himself from the sea's embrace, dress quickly, and head to Beach Road. There he bought two bottles of water and a shwarma.

He walked down Beach Road, eating and drinking, savouring the food, savouring doing something normal. He didn't look around him, didn't turn on his radar, did not scope for enemies who may or may have been near. For this time, just this brief time, he wanted to act like any other normal boy. He thought of his aunt and uncle, just a quarter of a mile away, pining for their daughter, worrying for him too. Bereft and terrified. There is no other way, he told himself, and took some consolation from the fact he was right, but still his heart ached.

He returned to Shell Beach, sat on the sand and finished his shwarma and water. He dumped the rubbish in a bin, then moved to the water's edge. He sat cross-legged, staring out into the tumbling waves and he called to the Sea Djinn of the Light.

Triton. I am here on Shell Beach. I need to see you. Please come.

As the sun rose to the midpoint, Finn sat and waited.

CHAPTER EIGHTY THREE

A Splinter
in the Heart

FINN FELT, MORE THAN saw, Triton's presence. He waded out into the sea, dived down underneath, opened his eyes and saw the Sea Djinn, waiting in the deeper water, eyes gleaming like emeralds.

Triton greeted Finn with a bow.

'Shall we go to the Cave of Light?' he asked, communicating telepathically with Finn.

Finn nodded. 'Yes, please.'

'Will you need to breathe above water?'

Finn assessed himself. Had he recovered enough? Would he let the shadow of death dictate to him?

Finn shook his head. 'I will breathe my own air underwater,' he communicated. He rose above the surface, breathed in deep, luxurious lungfulls of briny air. He imagined his powers rising from him. Even here, treading water in the sea, he could project them, was mindful of where his body stopped and where the water began. He pushed out the boundary, hardening it, sealing it. He dived back down underwater, moulding his boundaries so that he could sit astride Triton's broad back. He leaned forward, gripped round Triton's neck, held tight when the Sea Djinn flipped his massive tail and shot them out into deeper water.

They swam, blindingly fast, Finn taking small breaths when he needed to. Scything through the water, Finn felt more of the Blackness wash off him.

They swam through the ocean, then down into the Cave of Light. Triton waved his fingers back and forth before Finn's eyes and handed him the meteoric stone to keep him grounded.

Finn saw a rim of blackness still outline his aura, like a pencil drawing. So did Triton.

'A Death Mantle,' the Sea Djinn communicated, voice high with horror.

Triton raised his hands over Finn's head. Light poured from them like liquid gold. Finn felt it run down over him, down his head, down his neck, shoulders, arms, chest, stomach and back, down his legs, onto his feet. Finn felt bathed in Light. He felt the power of it pour into him.

He saw the dark outline crack and splinter. He watched it drift away into the water and dissolve in the brine. Yet he felt as if it had not quite all gone. He had the strangest sensation, as if a splinter of it had lodged in his heart.

Finn banished the thought, tuned into Triton who was communicating with him.

'Finn, my Boy, my child, what happened to you?

Unable to suppress a shudder, Finn told him.

'Bless Georgie and Fred for saving your life,' communicated Triton. '*Damn* the Spirit. *Damn* Typhon.' The water became turbulent, whipped up by Triton's anger.

'What did the Spirit of Darkness say,' asked Triton, icy control subduing the water around them.

Finn told Triton about the warnings of enemies.

'So now I wonder, who are these enemies close to me?' he communicated. 'Hawkman, but who else?'

Triton gazed out of the Cave of Light. For a long time, he said nothing.

'The picture is blurred. I cannot See. What I can discern are swirling images, unreadable.'

'Winds,' communicated Finn.

'It could be winds. It could be Shamal. It could even be Zephyr, though I do not think so. He is a Djinn of the Light, remember.'

Finn nodded, but he did not feel entirely convinced.

'But you would do well to be on your guard. More than ever,' communicated Triton. 'Now to your plan. I think Typhon will find the Burial Shroud and the Book of the Dead irresistible. You will be able to lure him to you with those Talismans and trade them for Mistral. That's step one. But for step two to work, you will have to block your thoughts. He will try to See into your mind. He will search for any attempt to outwit him. For your plan to succeed, he must have no idea of what is in your mind.'

'I will build a wall,' communicated Finn, 'and I will block him.'

Triton nodded.

'Do that. May victory and luck be yours.' Triton's eyes blazed, fierce with war and with love.

Finn's eyes burned too with emotion. He would win. He had no intention of entertaining death again for a good many decades.

Triton pointed to the meteoric rock in Finn's hand.

'Take this,' he said. He told Finn how to use it. 'Then flee with all speed,' concluded Triton.

'I will,' communicated Finn, 'like the devil himself were after me.'

He will be, thought Triton.

CHAPTER EIGHTY FOUR

❧ The Deal is Made ❧

F INN KEPT HIS WORD. He arrived back before sunset. He found Fred and Georgie standing in the courtyard staring up at the battlements.

'You're back. Thank goodness,' breathed Georgie. Finn nodded, glanced up at movement above.

He saw Shamal silhouetted against the setting sun, his kandoora billowing gently. He was reaching his arms up to the sky, holding them out, frozen. His movements were jerky, stressed.

'Looks like Mistral's communicating with Shamal,' said Fred.

Finn felt a surge of hope and of dread. Had Typhon been offered the trade? Had he accepted?

'I wonder what Shamal is saying back,' said Georgie, eyes narrowed in suspicion.

'Let's go and see,' said Finn. 'And remember, Shamal saved our lives.'

Georgie grunted, while Fred uttered a more sympathetic, 'Mhm.'

They ascended the spiral staircase, emerging dizzy at the top. Shamal stood at the far end of the battlements. They could feel Zephyr hovering around him. They could see the Storm Djinn in the shimmering air.

Shamal turned and gave them a dazzling smile, his eyes crinkling with warmth and respect. Finn felt a quick burn of shame, wished he didn't have to suspect someone who had always behaved, outwardly anyway, as a friend.

'Typhon has agreed!' declared Shamal triumphantly. 'The Burial Shroud and the Book of the Dead, delivered by Finn, in exchange for Mistral!'

'Where?' asked Georgie, voice sharp, wondering who or what was the bait. Was it the Burial Shroud and the Book of the Dead, or was it Finn?

'How will we ensure that Finn returns too, not just Mistral?' she asked.

'I will take Finn to the meeting place. I will bring him back here,' boomed Zephyr, voice echoing through the battlements. 'You have my word.'

Georgie studied the shimmering air. She wished she could see Zephyr's eyes, search in them for the truth, for any hint of duplicity.

'That's half the objective, isn't it,' said Finn, 'freeing Mistral, but there's the second half of the plan too,' he reminded Zephyr. 'Defeating Typhon once and for all. Stopping him from his mission to defeat you and to kill us three,' he added, gesturing to himself and Georgie and Fred.

'So tell me,' intoned Zephyr. 'How do you think we can do that?'

Finn told him.

There was an electric silence. Finn could feel the energy crackling around Zephyr.

The Storm Djinn's voice, when he spoke, was low like rumbling thunder, heavy with hatred for his ancient enemy.

'That will be a suitable waste ground,' he growled. 'It is a brilliant idea, Finn. You think like a Djinn.'

No, thought Finn, veiling his mind. *I think like a human. Don't underestimate us.* But he said nothing, chastened by the lust for vengeance he felt swirling in the wind.

'Then that is settled,' said Zephyr. 'That is what we shall do.'

'When?' asked Georgie.

'The day after tomorrow, at sunrise,' said Shamal.

Twenty four hours, thought Finn. 'Where?' he asked, voice grim.

'In the Dark Kingdom,' replied Shamal. 'In Typhon's Storm Fortress.'

CHAPTER EIGHTY FIVE

❧ The Fire Djinn ❧

FINN'S MIND WAS IN turmoil. That night, after dinner, he went up alone to the battlements. The Storm Fortress. Typhon's Dark Kingdom. Why there? What new unearthly powers would Typhon display in his own Kingdom? And why the delay? What was Typhon setting up in the meantime?

Too late, Finn told himself. The clock was ticking. He could almost hear it resounding in his head, tick tock, tick tock, counting down the seconds. He paced back and forth up in the battlements, gazing at the dark sky as if seeking an answer in the cold implacability of the stars.

While Finn paced and Fred studied the Book of the Dead, Georgie made her way down the long spiral staircase. Her bare feet made no sound. The only sign of her passage was the flickering of the torches that burned in holders fixed to the walls every twenty steps.

Georgie trailed her fingers above them, warmed by them, comforted by their soft light.

She came out into a deserted courtyard. At one end the brazier burned. She made her way towards it. A camel saddlebag lay to one side. Georgie sat on it and gazed about her, breathing in the scent of the incense that smouldered gently amongst the burning charcoal.

Above her, the stars burned with fierce beauty. The night lay like a black velvet cloak around her, soft, comforting. She stared into the flames, mesmerised by them. They flickered red, orange and gold. She looked deeper, her mind going into itself, down into the realms of the subconscious, where the power lay.

She smiled. Time to invoke. She stared harder at the flames, called out in her mind, focused all her being on the summoning.

She was so deep down in her subconscious, she jumped when the voice spoke from the flames.

'You called me,' it said, voice rich and slow.

Georgie smiled.

'Hello Vulcan. I did.'

The Fire Djinn of the Light smiled back at her, his lips a darker red than the flames, his eyes a sapphire, blue, brilliant and glittering.

Georgie felt her Fire Stone glow against her skin. She reached out her hand. Vulcan reached out his and clasped hers. His hand was warm. The flames did not burn her. But she felt heat in the power that surged through her.

'So tell me, my brave LightFighter, what can I do for you?'

Georgie told him. 'The day after tomorrow Finn goes to meet Typhon in the Dark Storm Fortress.'

Vulcan's fire flared red. He tried and failed to mask the foreboding in his eyes.

'What can I do to help?' he asked, voice grim.

Georgie told Vulcan the plan, told him what she needed from him. 'You can do that, can't you?' she asked, voice impassioned.

Vulcan nodded. 'It is my pleasure and my heritage. I will do all I can to help Finn in this battle. Give me this night and the day which follows.'

'Thank you,' said Georgie, hand reaching out to touch the Fire Djinn.

She hesitated as thoughts, fears fluttered through her mind. 'Vulcan, before you go. Is there any news about Jehannem? He's still dead, isn't he? I mean he hasn't reappeared.'

Vulcan's eyes turned grave again. 'No. He has not reappeared.'

'So he's dead?'

Vulcan hesitated. 'If he were dead, then a new Dark Fire Djinn should be emerging.'

'Has one emerged?'

'Not yet. Not to my knowledge.'

Georgie shuddered in spite of the warmth. 'But that means….'

'Not necessarily. Jehannem might be dead. It might just be that it is taking the new Dark Fire Djinn a long time to emerge. He might be keeping quiet somewhere, building his strength. He would be young, remember. He might not want to go screaming round the planet, causing trouble. At least, not yet.'

Georgie's eyes narrowed. 'What do you think?' she asked.

'There is a saying amongst you humans, sufficient unto the day is the evil thereof.'

'Which means?' asked Georgie.

'Worry about what is here and now. Not about what might be. What Finn will face tomorrow is more than enough to occupy all your worries.'

CHAPTER EIGHTY SIX

ೲ Chainmail ೲ

FINN TRAINED AGAIN WITH Zephyr the next day. He re-joined Georgie and Fred for dinner in the courtyard. Shamal sat with them too. Zephyr blew restively, cooling them, but disturbing them too. They could all feel his agitation.

They ate little, nerves grinding their stomachs, making it hard to swallow.

Georgie jumped up suddenly, grabbing her fire stone. She hurried across to the smouldering brazier.

She stood before it, examining it intently.

Finn watched her, then suddenly looked up, his eyes caught by a movement in the sky.

'Wow!' he breathed. 'Look at that.'

Blazing through the sky was a meteor. It was blue gold, with a golden orange tail that blazed out behind it. It was so dazzling it lit up the night.

'Have you ever seen anything so beautiful,' exclaimed Fred, eyes wide with wonder.

'It's coming this way,' gasped Shamal. 'It's heading right for us.'

Georgie smiled. 'So it is. Relax.'

Shamal raised an eyebrow. 'We're about to be incinerated and you say *relax?'*

'Yes,' giggled Georgie, eyes shining with delight.

Zephyr fell still, watching and waiting.

The meteor burned through the Heavens, heading relentlessly towards them. Suddenly it focused into a pinpoint and before they could blink it alighted in the courtyard.

The pinpoint of fire blazed into a shimmering column of blue, tinged with gold. Towards the top, eyes glowed at them and lips of blue fire smiled at them.

'Lord of the Storms. Forgive my entry uninvited.'

The air rippled and Finn felt Zephyr move.

'Fire Djinn of the Light, know you are welcome in the Castle of the Winds.'

'Thank you. And this child is part of you, is he not?' asked Vulcan, looking at Shamal.

'My son,' replied Zephyr, voice rich with pride and love.

'Greetings,' said Vulcan, holding out a narrow flame to Shamal. Gingerly Shamal reached out towards it, closer and closer until his fingers closed around it.

'You don't burn!' he exclaimed.

'Not friends and allies, no.'

Fred, Georgie and Finn watched the exchange with interest.

Vulcan moved towards Georgie. He bowed. 'Greetings, Georgina.'

Georgie bowed back. 'Hello Vulcan,' she said.

Finn and Fred, still trapped by the beauty of the meteor, remembered their manners just in time. They both bowed deeply.

'Hello Vulcan,' they chorused.

The fiery shape shimmered towards them.

'Fred, my rescuer. Greetings. And Finn, the Prince of Atlantis, greetings to you.'

'Did you bring it?' asked Georgie, unable to contain herself.

Vulcan smiled at her. He turned back to the shimmer of air that was Zephyr. 'I was summoned by our friend here. Commissioned too.' The flames glowed green for a moment, then an arm of flame emerged. From the arm hung a glittering shimmer of gold. Vulcan handed it to Finn.

'It is yours. Please, take it.'

Finn reached out. His fingers closed around gold, warm gold. He held it up.

'A chain mail cloak,' he said in wonder. 'Made of gold.'

'Put it on,' urged Vulcan.

Finn slipped his arms into it. It fell to the floor. He turned a slow circle. It shimmered and flowed as he moved, a cobweb mesh of gold.

'How can it be so light?' Finn asked.

'I smelted it so,' answered Vulcan.

'It's fabulous,' said Georgie. 'Like a work of art.'

Vulcan bowed. 'Thank you. There's more.' He reached into himself and drew out a pair of chain mail gloves, shoes of gold, and a special head-dress, with a visor to cover the eyes.

Finn put them all on.

Fred gasped in amazement. 'You look like a medieval knight, no, make that a medieval king, ready for battle.'

Finn smiled. Behind the visor his eyes glinted with purpose.

'That's what I am. Ready for battle.'

'It will protect you from Typhon's Dark Energy,' said Georgie.

'And he won't be able to locate you,' enthused Fred as realisation dawned. 'If you need to hide from him, the gold will block your magnetism. It's brilliant!' he shouted.

Vulcan smiled. He reached out and gently removed Finn's gloves, laying them on the floor beside him. He held Finn's hands, leaned in close and spoke so that only Finn could hear.

'Wear it well,' said Vulcan. 'It has enchantment in it. It is imbued with Light Fire. It will deflect evil. But it is only for you to wear. No-one else.' He straightened up and raised his voice, but still he kept Finn's hands gripped in his. 'Good luck, Finn. May you defeat Typhon and return to us.'

Finn felt the warmth and the power surge through him. He harnessed them, every spark of them. He nodded. 'Thank you Vulcan, for this,' he gestured to his chain mail, 'and for coming. I will return,' he added determinedly. 'I quite like my world.'

Vulcan let go of his hands.

'May the power of Light Fire show your way, sear your enemies, warm your friends.'

Vulcan turned to Georgie and Fred, touched them too, made his farewell to Shamal and finally, with a deep bow, to Zephyr. There was a flare as Fire met Wind and Finn felt a tremor of the power that the meeting of the two elements released. He wondered what it would be like if they fought side by side, Fire and Wind. What powers would be unleashed? For good, or for evil, because if the Light Djinns of Fire and Storm could fight together, then so could the Dark Djinns.

They all watched as the fire coalesced into a point. Then the point soared away. After a minute, it became a meteor once more, with a glorious flaming tail. They watched it fly up into the Heavens, lighting the night. They watched it until it disappeared, back into its own kingdom. Then, once again, the Castle of the Winds was dark, the only light the stars and the burning coals in the brazier.

CHAPTER EIGHTY SEVEN

Robed for Death or Armed for Life

FINN, FRED AND GEORGIE headed across the court-yard to the spiral staircase that would take them to the Safe Room.

Zephyr drifted up.

'Finn, a moment, if I may?' he asked.

Georgie and Fred moved on reluctantly.

'Your chainmail is magnificent,' commented Zephyr.

Finn nodded.

'Something troubles you, oh Prince. Tell me.'

Finn sagged slightly. He could feel Zephyr around him, intent, concerned, quietly implacable. He *would* know.

'It's my chainmail. It's a present, a glorious one, made from love and a wish to protect. And I can see the logic, see that it will mask me.' Finn faltered.

'It's just that it looks like Tutankhamen's Burial Shroud.'

'That's why they did it,' answered Zephyr.

Finn's eyes widened. 'The Ancient Egyptians? To pro-tect the dead from the ravages of a Djinn?'

'Not just of a Djinn, of Typhon, seeking them out, seeking to steal their secrets as they passed from Life to Death and on to Eternal Life in the Netherworld. Even then they knew they had to block him,' explained Zephyr.

'So I will go to Typhon clothed for death?' asked Finn.

'No!' replied Zephyr. 'You have three presents now, from three Djinn Lords of the Light. And you have your own powers too, Finn. You will go into this battle armed for Life.'

Chapter Eighty Eight

❦ Enchanted Sleep ❦

FINN DRAPED THE CHAINMAIL over a camel saddle-bag in the Safe Room. It gleamed at him in the darkness. Fred and Georgie were asleep, or pretending to be, each locked in their own thoughts and fears which no-one wanted to communicate. Fred *was* asleep, realised Finn. He lay thrashing, muttering, caught in the grip of a nightmare.

Finn lay down to sleep. He thought of the Dark Meniscus, of Typhon's Storm Fortress, of the Dark Kingdom awaiting him. He thought of his enemies. He had killed Jehannem. He had captured Hydrus. He would vanquish Typhon too.

Finn fell into what seemed to him to be an enchanted sleep. He was asleep but oddly conscious at the same time. He was aware of his body repairing and strengthening as he slept, as if something from Vulcan's chainmail had permeated his body. He felt his cells renew, felt them go beyond renewal becoming something more than they had been before. When he awoke at dawn, his muscles felt like tensile steel.

CHAPTER EIGHTY NINE

∽ Sacrifice ∽

'IT IS TIME,' SAID Zephyr as dawn broke the next day.

Finn picked up his chainmail and began to thread his arm through one sleeve.

'Finn!' shouted Fred. 'I knew there was something. I dreamed about it last night. I don't think you can push out your force-field when you're wearing your chainmail. I think it'll block it, so you need to create your force-field then put on your chainmail.'

Finn's eyes widened with shock. 'Better put it to the test,' he said. He pulled on the chainmail, golden shoes, helmet and visor too. He closed his eyes, focused inward, drew on his powers, pushed them out from his heart in a flood of light. He reached out to feel for his force-field. His fingers floundered in air. He swore loudly. *Robed for death*, said the voice in his mind. *Shut up!* He told it.

Sweating, he carefully removed his chain mail and laid it on the low table. Then he took a few breaths, closed his eyes, calmed himself and went into himself again. He summoned his energy once more, poured it out, pushed it around him. He reached out his fingers, suppressing the fear that tried to find voice: *What if you can't do it, now that you really need to? Focus*, he told himself. And *believe*. He recalled Mr Violet's voice. *You can do it, Finn, you know you can. Believe. Just believe!* His fingers found the boundary. He pushed it out further, filled it with air. Then he crystallised it.

'Fred. I am going to resist you,' said Finn. 'Try to push through.'

'OK.' Fred approached Finn, reached out his palm and pushed. His hand stopped in mid air, two feet from Finn's body.

'Phew,' said Finn. He reached for his chainmail, pulled it through his force-field, robed himself from head to toe. Finn walked an experimental circle, getting used to the feel of his armour. Wearing it, he did feel different. He did feel a bit like a medieval knight. He felt a new power too. Vulcan's enchantment. Finn could feel it shimmering against him. The chainmail felt alive.

'Try again,' he asked Fred. His voice sounded echoey through the head-dress and visor.

Fred reached out, again found Finn's force-field, got no further.

'That was a pretty useful dream, Fred,' said Finn.

'Too flippin' right,' agreed Georgie.

Finn picked up his backpack containing the Book of the Dead, the Burial Shroud and the meteoric rock that Triton had given him.

'You look a true Prince. Robed for Life,' declared Zephyr.

Finn nodded.

'Are you ready?' asked the Djinn Lord.

'I am,' replied Finn. He looked at Georgie and Fred. He lifted up his visor so that he could see them better.

Georgie stepped forward, face fierce. 'See you later, then, Finn. Good luck.'

Finn nodded, eyes fixed on Georgie's, acknowledging all the things left unsaid. 'See you later, George.'

Fred stepped up as Georgie moved back. 'Bye, mate. Good luck. Not that you need it, but it always helps.'

'Always,' replied Finn. 'Thanks, mate. Catch you later.'

Shamal came up to him, face grave. 'I will thank you when you return, but I send my thanks too in advance. For your bravery. For your sacrifice.'

Finn's blood chilled. 'It is no *sacrifice*. I shall return unharmed. Unless you know something.' He took a step towards Shamal, eyes blazing.

Shamal stood his ground as Finn's force-field buffeted him.

'I cannot read the future,' replied Shamal.

Finn leaned forward towards him. 'That's no answer. But know this. I will *make* the future,' he hissed. 'Without sacrifice.'

Georgie and Fred watched, mouths dry as dust.

Finn wheeled around and shut down his visor. He felt Zephyr building his power. The wind picked up speed.

'Remember my warning, Finn. Do not be seduced by what you will see,' said Zephyr, voice grave. 'There is no stopping.'

Finn nodded. His mind was filled with wonderful visions of the journey to come. He would see horrors, he would see sights for which many men would sell their soul. And he would return, if all went well. If it did not, then he would be lost in time, stranded forever. He smiled. This would be the journey to end all journeys.

CHAPTER NINETY

The Dark
Storm Fortress

T HE WIND SCREAMED THROUGH the battlements. Finn felt it hauling at him, fighting the gravity that kept him grounded, winning effortlessly. He soared into the sky. He watched the Castle of the Winds shrink below him until Georgie, Fred and Shamal faded into invisibility. The expanse of the Rub al Khali rolled out below in all its dread magnitude. Then the wind blew faster, wilder until the desert and the air became a blur.

Finn flew through space like a bullet. He smiled to himself. That is what I am, Typhon, I am a bullet and I am heading for your heart.

Zephyr flew faster still. Inside his golden armour, Finn felt the tumult squeeze his body, but the force was nothing like last time. The armour and his own force-field, stronger now, protected him.

It seemed to Finn that they were flying into space because the air grew dark around them and they flew faster still as if there were no atmosphere to slow them. He should have been cold, but the golden armour, forged by Vulcan, imbued with his cool fire, warmed him.

Abruptly, everything changed. Finn felt as if they had entered a chasm and were in free fall. Down they went, falling, twisting, spinning, sucked towards some awful magnet.

The Dark Kindgom. Finn knew it by its feel. Dread and despair. Evil. A Darkness not of repair and restoration but of annihilation of Light, of Goodness.

But the Darkness was not quite absolute. As they hurtled downwards, Finn saw the Fortress below them. They were approaching it like a rocket. Black it was, like granite, following the contours of a mountaintop, the monstrous walls rising and falling, their battlements cutting into the deadly air. In seconds they would hit it, pulverise themselves against it. Was this how it was going to end, wondered Finn, in what he realised was probably his last thought; a crash and then oblivion?

'Stooop!' he screamed to Zephyr. The wind, the screaming maddening howl of it stole his words.

They stopped. Stopping was like a collision between motion and stillness.

The ground swam before Finn's feet. He staggered and stumbled. He straightened quickly, stood like a medieval knight, readied himself. He breathed in his own air, sipping it slowly, making it last. He gazed around, but could see nothing in the night-pitched gloom.

Beside him he felt Zephyr coiling slowly, gathering himself.

A howling wind tore through the blackness. It came closer, closer, till Finn saw in the darkness and the maelstrom a pair of eyes. He stared in horror. There was no body, just a profound darkness, spiralling in on itself, like a black hole. And, like a black hole, it seemed to be drawing him towards it, pulling him in like some satanic gravity.

He had felt Typhon before, been battered in his midst, but never had he looked into his eyes, seen his black heart.

The maelstrom spoke.

'So you come, Zephyr, bearing gifts.'

'So we have come,' replied Zephyr. 'Not with gifts, but with our trade. Where is Mistral?'

Typhon said nothing. Finn fancied he could hear a beat coming from the heart of him, from the black hole; a deep thud, thud, thud. Despite his golden armour, he felt himself being sucked towards Typhon.

'You wear the Burial Shroud?' hissed Typhon, eyes razing up and down Finn's body.

'No. The Shroud is in here,' said Finn, gesturing to his backpack.

'You wear chainmail to protect yourself against me,' mused Typhon. 'Do you think it will?'

'Yes,' replied Finn. 'I think it will.'

'As a plaster would protect you from a chainsaw,' observed Typhon. 'You have the Book of the Dead?'

'In the backpack,' replied Finn.

'Bring us Mistral,' commanded Zephyr. 'I know you are desperate for company Typhon, but our Kingdoms wait.'

'Hm, and those would be the Kingdom of Light and the Kingdom of Atlantis?'

'The Kingdom of Earth,' replied Finn. 'That is where I belong.'

Typhon laughed. 'Is that what you think?'

A thunderclap rolled round the battlements.

Finn saw a shimmer of movement. He felt Zephyr suck in a breath. Moving towards them was a girl, robed like Finn. Her dark hair fell outside her golden chainmail, and on her helmet, where Finn had a visor, she had strands of gold raining down her face, mixing with a black fringe.

The dark mass that was Typhon shifted. Mistral, as if physically restrained, froze.

'Show me the Talismans. Now!' ordered Typhon.

Finn removed his backpack, opened it carefully. First he withdrew the Burial Shroud. He held it up. As he did so, Finn felt the Shroud almost wrenched from his hands by Typhon's Dark Energy. He gripped it fiercely as Typhon stared at it. He seemed to be assessing every link of its fibre. Finally, the Dark Djinn nodded. 'The Book of the Dead?'

Finn put away the Burial Shroud and removed the Book of the Dead. He held it up to Typhon. He felt the surge of power again, the dark gravity, pulling him and the Book in. He fought it, streaming with sweat at the effort.

'Come,' commanded Typhon.

Mistral began to move. She got closer. She was Shamal's height and like her brother, she was slight of build. She moved with mesmeric grace. She stopped just feet from Finn. He saw the gleam of her dark eyes watching him. Beside him he heard Zephyr exhale.

'Mistraaaaal. ' He breathed her name in a lament of love and sorrow and joy. The girl fell forwards into her father's embrace. Her feet lifted off the ground and she closed her eyes.

'Mistral…Mistral….' intoned Zephyr, breathing her in. Mistral said nothing.

'The trade,' boomed Typhon.

Zephyr stilled. 'All in good time. First I will take Mistral from you, back to my own Kingdom.'

Finn gasped. This was not part of the plan.

'I shall take the backpack with me, Finn,' said Zephyr. 'With the Book of the Dead and the Burial Shroud. When

I have taken Mistral home, then I shall return. Only then shall you have your Talismans, Typhon.'

'You do not trust me?' asked Typhon, derisive laughter in his voice.

'No. Of course not.'

'But you will leave the Prince here, as my hostage?'

'Not as a hostage. As a guarantee of my return.' Fingers of wind stretched out to Finn. He gripped the backpack tightly. Should he give it to Zephyr? Should he hang onto it? He built a wall round his mind. He did not want Zephyr looking in. He could not afford for Typhon to look in. He calculated furiously. If Zephyr wanted to betray him, to kill him, then he would be no match for both he and Typhon who assuredly did want to kill him to stop the Travellers' Prophecy from ever coming true. All he could do was to go along with Zephyr and pray he was telling the truth.

Finn felt like screaming, like shouting out: *this is not what we agreed.*

Zephyr turned to Finn.

'I will be back. I promise. Trust me.'

Wordlessly, Finn handed over the backpack. He watched Mistral walk away with Zephyr coiling around her. Further away they moved, so they would not take Finn with them, carried in the slipstream, he realised.

But Finn still felt the wind build, heard the roar of it, felt the yank of it as Mistral shot into the air, golden chainmail shimmering. Finn watched her soar up through the darkness like a shooting star. He watched until she disappeared.

The roar of the wind faded. A dreadful silence descended. Stretched from seconds to minutes.

Finn waited, entombed by silence.

CHAPTER NINETY ONE

✆ Betrayal? ✆

FINN FELT TYPHON'S EYES upon him.

'So, you're wondering now, aren't you, oh Prince, whether he'll come back, the Djinn of the Light. Perhaps he is not quite completely of the Light. Have you thought of that? We Storm Djinns twist and turn so, do we not?' suggested Typhon, his voice evilly sibilant.

Typhon spoke Finn's fears. Spoke Triton's warning.

'Why are you so intent on getting all the Talismans? Why do you lust so after a power that you will never have?' Finn asked, goading the Dark Djinn.

'But I *will* have the power. With the Talismans I will defeat Zephyr. Then I shall have his gift. I shall be able to travel through Time, back and forth.'

'But his gift involves respecting the Sacred Covenant. He can travel through Time but he is forbidden to change the past.'

Typhon's laughter rolled out like machine-gun fire.

'Covenants are there to be broken.'

'Why? You already have more than enough power. Why can't you be satisfied with moulding the present, per-haps even making it better, rather than worse.'

'There is no day without night, no light without dark,'

replied Typhon.

'So you are telling me that you are a necessary evil. Is that right?' asked Finn.

'Cosmic balance.'

'I don't think so. I think that's just a convenient excuse for evil. Night is for growth and replenishment, not for evil.'

'You have a brain, Prince. Shame to have to destroy it.'

'You never will,' hissed Finn.

'Oh, I can See the fear in your soul. You know you have been abandoned here. Betrayed. *You* are the Sacrifice. Don't you know? Mistral in exchange for you. A good deal, I must say.'

Finn's heart began to pound. *Where* was Zephyr.

'Perhaps I could use you as I used her. Keep you in the leaden room. Bring you out when I need the benefit of that brain. Or when I feel bored.' Typhon swirled around Finn. 'But maybe not. You are, after all, prophesied to kill me. To make me disappear. It might not be wise to allow you to live.'

Finn tried to block out his words and the fear that was building in his heart. Was this the betrayal that the Spirit of Darkness had warned him of? Had he so blindly walked into a trap? He felt his force-field waiver as doubts assailed him.

He slammed the doubts away. He filled his mind with all that was good. He recalled the feel of the sea sluicing off his body as he surfed the waves. He recalled the Cave of Light and breathing his own air underwater. He recalled Georgie and Fred. *I will get out of this,* he thought. *I will outwit you.*

'Will you now?' demanded Typhon, reading Finn's thoughts as surely as if he had spoken them aloud. 'I think not,' he said.

Finn called down a wall of sand in his mind, blocking his thoughts. Typhon laughed. 'So you think you can block me, do you? I can cut into your brain like a laser. Just watch. That will be as good a way as any to kill you.'

Finn primed his force-field, hardened it. In response, the wind picked up, screamed through the air.

Finn stood motionless, trapped in the vortex.

CHAPTER NINETY TWO

Journey to End All Journeys

ᴇᴘʜʏʀ ʟᴇғᴛ Mɪsᴛʀᴀʟ ᴡɪᴛʜ Shamal in the Castle of the Winds. He took with him the backpack containing the Burial Shroud, the Book of the Dead and the meteoric rock. Georgie and Fred watched it vanish in seconds as Zephyr soared off through the sky, into the heavens. They could see the clouds billowing wildly, marking his passing.

In minutes, Zephyr was back with Finn and Typhon. Finn stood in the vortex, eyes shut, concentrating with all his powers. Typhon had not broken through. Finn felt a surge of elation. He felt Zephyr return, felt the Light return. Typhon ceased his torment.

'So you have returned, Zephyrrrr,' said the Dark Djinn, rolling the r in disgust.

'As promised,' replied Zephyr. The backpack hovered in the centre of his shimmering mass.

'So. Give me the Book. Give me the Shroud.'

'Not here,' replied Zephyr. 'Not in your Kingdom.'

Typhon roared. 'You would disobey me? In my own Kingdom?'

'I would never obey you in any Kingdom,' replied Zephyr. 'We will leave your Kingdom together, the three of us, in peace. Then, once we are outside your Kingdom, we shall give you what you seek.'

'And how do I know that you can be trusted?' hissed Typhon.

'Because I am a Djinn of the Light. I keep my word.'

'How pious you are,' sneered Typhon.

'Are you ready?' asked Zephyr. Finn felt the question was for him. He flicked a glance at where he thought Zephyr's eyes were, smiled in answer. He saw a glimmer flash back at him. He reached into the shimmering mass and withdrew the backpack. He pulled it on over his chainmail. Part One of the plan had been accomplished. Now it was time for Part Two.

'I am ready,' growled Typhon.

Zephyr accelerated like a rocket from the ground. Finn shot up with him, stomach lurching. It felt as if it would burst from his mouth. Up they screamed through the dark air. Finn could feel the awful gravity pulling him back down to the Dark Fortress. No wonder Zephyr had shot off so fast. He knew if he didn't they would never attain escape velocity. They would be stuck in the Dark Kingdom forever. He saw the black mass rearing up through the air beside them. Typhon. Finn saw the black eyes, gleaming through the eternal night.

Up they went, further and further. Finn felt an overwhelming pressure, then they exploded out from the Dark Kingdom. He saw the distant sun. He saw the Dark Meniscus form around it. He heard Typhon's voice, screaming above the wind.

'My Talismans. Now!'

Then he heard Zephyr's laughter. 'Soon. Soon. First, Dark Lord, we are going for a trip. A trip you have always wanted to take.'

At that, Zephyr summoned all his powers and accelerated beyond all the barriers of Time.

Finn felt a bending and a snapping, heard the explosion, heard Typhon's roar of rage, then his gasp.

Down below them, were the bands of Time. Finn saw them spooling, round and round the earth. He saw medieval castles, knights robed not unlike himself, galloping far below on armed chargers. He saw once again the pyramids. He saw ancient jungles with monumental stone palaces rising from them. He saw volcanoes erupt. He saw the sea, so green, so blue, so beautiful. His heart lurched. He saw below the sea the outline of buildings. He focused his eyes, sent all his consciousness down and he Saw. He saw a city, he saw humans swimming between buildings. He saw children swimming, playing with sea creatures. The name shot into his head. Atlantis! He was looking at his home. That could have been him, swimming with the dolphins, playing with sea horses that frolicked underwater, riding their backs, gripping their watery manes. And he would breathe. He could feel it. His soul called out to them. His heart cried out to them. He felt them looking up at him. He was getting lower, getting closer. Soon he would plunge into the silken water. He would join the children, join his ancestors. His skin quivered. He was ready. This was it. This was what he had searched for all his life without knowing it. He felt a yearning so strong he felt torn in half.

'Fiiiiiiiin!' roared a voice, shattering his mind. 'Fiiiiiin. Stop. You cannot go there. Not here. Not now!'

Zephyr! thought Finn. He remembered Zephyr's warning.

You will see sights to end all sights. You will want to stop but if you leap off the bands of Time, you will be lost in Time.

Finn watched the water, saw a woman. She looked like his mother, saw a man, just like his father, and a girl. Could have been his sister. He looked closer. It was his sister! *This was home,* screamed the voice in his head. *Come home. Come home.*

CHAPTER NINETY THREE

⊚ Trapped in Time ⊚

Z EPHYR'S WARNING ROLLED ROUND his head, matching the words the Storm Djinn was screaming: 'Finn! Finn! In the name of Light, hold fast. Remember your purpose.'

Finn tore his gaze from the water, lurched up and away. So close, so close the water had been whipped up into a storm. The sea splashed up, hit his face, drenched him. He licked his lips. Tasted the ancient salt. Remembered it. But they powered away. Up and away. Away from the water, away from Atlantis, away from his dream. He gasped, he screamed. It had been so close. Finn flew away, with tears coursing down his face.

They flew on through Time. He saw most of the planet blanketed by trees, so green, so beautiful. But nothing was as beautiful as Atlantis. Nothing ever was. Nothing ever could be.

Back they went, till all signs of human habitation were wiped from the surface of the earth. Back further, through Ice Ages, where a sheen of brilliant white dazzled him. Back further. Then he saw them and his eyes opened again with wonder. Great, lumbering beasts powering their way across endless savannahs. T Rexes, huge and terrifying. Herds of

Diplodocus, grazing peaceably. Packs of velociraptors hunting their prey, bringing them down. Finn could hear their war shrieks, terrifying. Merciless.

They were getting closer. Finn veiled his mind, readied himself. He stole a glance toward where Typhon rode with them, saw his eyes, avid, lit with a kind of joy. Finn felt a flash of humanity for him, banished it as he heard the velociraptors screaming again. He must be like them, merciless.

They were plummeting towards the ground. Finn strained and with super-human strength, he reached round, grabbed his backpack. He held it to his chest, felt around in it, found the meteoric rock, wrapped the Burial Shroud in it. He pulled it from the backpack, hurled it downwards. He followed it with the Book of the Dead, flinging it through the air. The wind ripped pages from it, shredding them.

Typhon screamed, a sound of primeval rage. He stormed down to earth, chasing the Burial Shroud. Zephyr turned, powered away from the earth. Finn felt the G force, worse than any he had experienced before. His eyes fluttered, he felt the blackness encroaching as he began to lose consciousness. He fought it as Zephyr hurtled upwards, accelerating madly. Finn struggled for breath. His air supply was running short, and as he fought for consciousness he was forced to suck in great lungs full of air.

Finn heard another scream. He looked down. He could see the swirling black mass of Typhon hurtling up towards them, roaring with fury and terror as he realised the trap into which he had been lured.

Zephyr was going so fast, too fast. Finn's body couldn't stand it. But he knew that if they slowed, Typhon would catch them, ride the Winds of Time with them and escape.

So Finn said nothing. He did not call for help, he did not scream to Zephyr to slow. Not as his breath failed and the blood burst from his eyes. But he would not die again. He fought it. His fingers found their way to his sea glass and his fire stone. He gripped them with all his strength. He took all they had.

His vision was blurring, but he saw they were in space again, flying over the bands of Time. They had left the dinosaurs behind. They had left Typhon behind. They had won. Now all he had to do was hang on. Hang on. Hang on……

Chapter Ninety Four

❧ Extinction Event ❧

EORGIE AND FRED PACED through the courtyard, eyes trained on the sky. They had seen the
Dark Meniscus form. Abruptly it disappeared.

'Look!' shouted Georgie. 'It's gone. The Dark
Meniscus.'

Fred screwed up his eyes and glanced at the sun. 'What
does that mean? I wonder if it?...' His words trailed off. The
clouds were racing. The storm was approaching. Seconds
later, it hit.

Zephyr landed in the courtyard. Finn emerged from
the folds of the storm. He staggered forward, his chainmail
clinking as he moved. Georgie and Fred ran to him. They
caught him as he fell.

Exhausted, he pushed up his visor. Blood coursed
down his face, but his eyes were triumphant.

'We did it,' he exclaimed. 'We trapped Typhon in
Time. Back with the dinosaurs.'

Fred and Georgie whooped.

'You did it! Finn you did it!'

'With a bit of help from Zephyr,' he said with a smile.
Zephyr shimmered around him.

'I could not have done it without you, Finn.'

'You trapped him in Time,' trilled Georgie in wonder. 'I'm still trying to get my head round it.'

'So that's why!' exclaimed Fred suddenly.

'Why what?' asked Finn.

'Why the dinosaurs became extinct. Typhon killed them all.'

CHAPTER NINETY FIVE

∞ Possession ∞

'MISTRAL,' MURMURED FINN. 'WHERE is she?' he asked, peeling off his chainmail and laying it carefully on the camel saddlebag by the brazier.

'Wow, she was something, arriving back here with her golden chainmail,' said Georgie. 'Not as fine as yours, not wrought by Vulcan of course, but she is so beautiful, and when she took it off she just stood there in rough trousers and a tee shirt and she still looked like a princess.'

Finn smiled. 'Where is she now?'

'Gone with Shamal. To see their mother, to see if she is - '

'Hareb!' shouted Finn. 'With Typhon banished Hareb might have woken up.'

The three of them hurried across the courtyard, ascended the spiral staircase to Hareb's room. They paused a moment before entering. Finn caught his breath, then opened the door.

Hareb lay prone, eyes staring at the ceiling.

'Noooo,' yelled Georgie, disappointment flooding her.

Very slowly, almost too slowly to follow, Hareb's eyes turned towards Georgie. She was too distraught to notice, but Finn and Fred did. They gasped.

'Hareb!' exclaimed Fred.

Georgie looked up, eyes widening with amazement.

'Hareb!' she cried, running over to him. She threw herself on him, hugged him hard.

Hareb did not speak, did not move. Georgie stepped back. Finn bent over his friend.

'We did it, Hareb!' declared Finn. 'We trapped Typhon in Time. He's back with the dinosaurs.'

Hareb's eyes darkened. He reached out his arms, beckoning Finn into his embrace. His arms snaked up Finn's back, up to his neck, and began to choke him. Finn struggled desperately but Hareb held him in a death grip.

Fred and Georgie fell upon Hareb, trying to wrench him off Finn. Drained of most of his strength, Finn writhed and fought but he could not pull free.

'You have trapped me!' roared Hareb. 'You have deceived me and you have trapped me!' He kicked out at them, murder in his eyes.

'You will pay! You will pay!' he screamed.

'Typhon has possessed him,' shouted Fred. 'Get out your sea glass and your fire stone,' he yelled to Georgie. 'Hold them to his wrists.'

Hareb roared in pain and in fury as the pendants touched his skin. He thrashed against them and let go of Finn.

Finn fell to the floor, eyes bulging, gasping in air through his choked throat.

'He's going to break free,' yelled Georgie.

Finn pushed himself up, reaching for his sea glass and firestone.

He tore open Hareb's shirt and held the glass and stone to his heart. Hareb bucked and screamed in agony. He glared back at Finn with Typhon's evil eyes.

Together, they held him down, held their pendants in place. Finn drew out his whistle and blew. Seconds ticked by. Then Zephyr was amongst them.

'Typhon has possessed him,' yelled Georgie.

Zephyr blew, he created a tornado in the room. He blew so hard Georgie was lifted off her feet. The wind screamed round and round and Hareb screamed on with it.

Suddenly, he fell silent. Zephyr slowed, then hovered in the room.

Hareb's eyes shut. For minutes, agonisingly long minutes, they watched him. His breathing slowed. Georgie feared it would stop altogether.

Abruptly, his eyes opened.

'Goodness!' he exclaimed. 'What on earth's going on?'

Georgie looked into his eyes, Hareb's eyes not Typhon's, and smiled. 'You're back.'

Hareb looked puzzled. 'Have I been somewhere? Where? Where have I been?'

CHAPTER NINETY SIX

⌾ Leila ⌾

'**O**H GOD,' EXCLAIMED FINN. 'What if it's happened to Shamal and Mistral's mother too? Mightn't she be possessed by Typhon?'

Zephyr, who had been slowly moving around the room, fell still.

'We must go, now, all of us.'

They dragged Hareb out into the courtyard on legs that did not want to work. Finn grabbed his chainmail. Zephyr spun and wheeled around them.

'Where are we going? And why?' asked Hareb.

'Later,' said Finn. 'There's no time to explain now.' There were some things, anyway, it was better not to know. He had no intention of telling Hareb that he had been possessed by Typhon.

Georgie, Finn, Fred and Hareb held hands, gripping on tightly as the air began to vibrate around them. Seconds later, their feet lifted off the ground and they shot into the sky.

Finn looked down at the Castle of the Winds, wondering if this were his last view of it, saying a quiet goodbye just in case.

They landed in the Rashid Hospital car park. They

were screened by the sand whipped up in the shamal Zephyr had created.

'Are you coming in with us?' Finn asked Zephyr.

The Djinn Lord hesitated. Finn could feel his uncertainty. 'I have caused her so much pain, so much trouble,' he intoned.

'Not you,' said Finn. 'Typhon.'

'Our war. The War of the Djinn. I am part of it. No. I will stay here and wait for Mistral and Shamal to come out. Summon me if you need me. If she is possessed.'

Finn nodded grimly. 'I will.'

Fred, Finn and Georgie rushed into the hospital. Hareb, bemused, limped slowly after them.

Leila Sultan was on the first floor. Room 303.

'Lots of visitors today,' said the smiling Receptionist. 'Her son and daughter and now you three.'

They ran up the stairs, down the long, antiseptic smelling, white corridor, to room 303.

They burst in without knocking. Mistral sat weeping. Finn nearly reeled backwards. Without her chain mail, he could see her face properly. She looked like Shamal, clearly his twin, but with the angular beauty of a woman. Shamal sat beside her. They looked up at Finn, Fred and Georgie with sorrowful eyes.

In the bed sat a beautiful woman, long, dark hair trailing to her waist. Or she would have been beautiful, thought Georgie, had it not been for the look in her eyes.

She was staring at Mistral and Shamal with a look of blazing intensity. It veered between hatred and desperation. Her eyes burned with it. She was jerking slightly as if she longed to move but was frantically trying to hold herself back.

'She's possessed by Typhon,' whispered Georgie, gently laying her hand on Mistral's shoulder. 'She cannot love you as she wants to.'

Mistral turned her huge eyes upon Georgie. 'To have this, to have her come back to life, and be....' she shuddered.

'We can get rid of Typhon,' whispered Finn.

The door opened again and Hareb limped in.

Shamal's eyes opened wide with pleasure and surprise.

'Hareb! You're here. You're normal!' he exclaimed, his eyes flickering back to his mother.

Hareb looked at Leila and flinched.

He had some recollection of feeling like she looked, of hating, of fighting the hate. He struggled, but the memory wouldn't come.

Finn turned to him. 'Hareb, could you please take Mistral and Shamal out for ten minutes?'

Hareb, Mistral and Shamal all looked at Finn in surprise.

'You need a coffee,' declared Georgie, determinedly. 'Go. Please,' she urged when no-one moved.

'Trust us,' said Fred.

Mistral and Shamal exchanged a look. Georgie could see the emotions warring in their eyes.

Shamal nodded to his twin. They headed for the door with a mixture of regret and relief.

'Do *not* come back before ten minutes,' whispered Finn to Hareb as they filed out.

Finn closed the door behind them. And locked it.

'Do not let anyone stop us,' he said softly. 'When we have started, we have to finish.'

Fred and Georgie nodded grimly.

In the absence of her daughter, the woman now turned her attention to Finn and Fred and Georgie. Her eyes flitted between them, like an animal sizing up its prey.

Finn raised his eyebrows as if to say: *ready?*

Georgie and Fred gave infinitesimal nods. Finn quickly wedged a chair under the door handle to jam it. They all reached for their sea glass and their firestones. Finn took his golden whistle and he blew. Together they leapt at the woman just as she leapt at Finn.

Chapter Ninety Seven

☙ Freedom ❧

LEILA DIDN'T SCREAM. SHE fought and she writhed and she turned her dark eyes upon them with looks of such corrosive hatred they would have quailed had they not been in the heat of battle themselves.

The door blew in, the chair hurtled across the room. Zephyr slammed the door shut behind him and swirled among them, creating his vortex. Papers spiralled in a mad frenzy. Finn, Fred and Georgie still gripped the lunging woman, keeping their pendants pressed to her skin. Zephyr blew the Blackness away. The firestones burned it away and the sea glass healed.

Finally, hair wild and tempest-tossed, Leila fell still. She leaned back against the bed, pushed her hair from her eyes. She glanced between them. Her eyes were puzzled now and wistful.

'Did I dream?' she said slowly. 'My daughter. My son. I saw them. I think I saw them. I – '

The door opened slowly. In walked Hareb, followed by Shamal and Mistral. Leila's eyes widened. She reached out her arms. Her children flew to her, fell into her embrace. Behind them, Zephyr meatamorphosed. He became a man. He stood in a white kandoora, robed over with a bisht. He was tall, regal-looking, eyes full of love and yearning. As if they felt his presence, Shamal and Mistral drew back from their mother and turned. The three of them saw him at once. They gasped, then shouted with joy, called to him, laughed and cried all in seconds.

Hareb turned to Finn, Fred and Georgie.

'Time to go?' he mouthed.

They nodded. Silently, they walked from the room, down the corridor, into the lift, then out of the hospital.

CHAPTER NINETY EIGHT

⚭ Augury ⚭

HAREB WENT TO HIS home. Finn and Georgie dropped off Fred at his, then headed for theirs.

Fred's mother screamed when she saw him and dropped the plant she was holding. It fell with its container to the marble floor and smashed noisily. Fred's mother leapt over the shards, grabbed Fred, drew him into an enormous bear hug, saying his name over and over. 'Freddie. Oh Freddie. Freddie. You're home. You're here.'

Finally, she released him, just as his father came barrelling into the room.

'Ali, I heard a crash - Freeeedieee!' he yelled, joy in his eyes. He grabbed his son, held him tight. They stood that way, the three of them, just holding on.

Georgie and Finn climbed over the wall and went into the house. It was a Saturday. Aunt C and Uncle Johnny were sitting with Cordelia and Cressida, all staring glassy eyed at a Scooby Doo cartoon.

Georgie cleared her throat.

Aunt C jumped, wheeled round, eyes enormous.

'Georgie!' she screamed. 'Finn!'

'Thank God!' yelled Uncle Johnny, jumping up. The twins screeched with joy and launched themselves at their sister. They even gave Finn a hug.

They celebrated quietly. They cooked dinner. They walked round the garden, they hugged. Finn and Georgie told Johnny everything that had happened. He listened, as they had known he would, with patience, making no comment until the end.

'My God!' he said, blowing out a huge breath. 'Your lives……' his voice trailed off as he struggled with his emotions. 'But you're home now,' he said decisively. 'It's over.'

When Finn went up to bed later he stood for a long while at his window, looking out at the night. The wind moaned through the palm trees outside on the street, restless. Forever restless. Like Finn himself. He moved from the window, stood before his wardrobe, eyeing his golden chainmail. It seemed to pulse, alive in the darkness; a memory of who he was, of what he had done. And an augury, he knew that, of what was to come. Finn knew that the battles were not over.

THE END

Grammatical and Historical Note

Scholars will know that djinn is the plural and djinni the singular. I have invoked artistic licence to spell both the same as I think it sounds better. There are alternate spellings - jinn (plural) and jinni (singular) and of course, the English but sometimes cliched-sounding genie.

Djinn are alluded to in both Christianity and Islam. The Holy Qur'an describes how Allah created two parallel species of creature; man and djinn, the one from clay, the other from fire. According to the Holy Qur'an, djinn are supernatural spirits below the level of angels (who were created from light) and demons.

Djinn can be good or evil. They can be visible or invisible and can shape shift, assuming human, animal and inanimate forms.

According to the Arabian Nights, Solomon was reputed to have mastered djinn, imprisoning them in sealed jars and throwing them into the sea.

Early Islamic belief suggested that shooting stars were darts thrown at djinn by angels, on whom they were attempting to eavesdrop.

Djinn are altogether rather wondrous creatures. Look out for them! Cunning humans who know the right charms, like Solomon, are said to be able to control them.

Acknowledgements

First, I would like to thank, as always, Isobel Abulhoul and Jane Hodges of Jerboa Books for their continued support of me and my writing and for their valuable input and enthusiasm. The rest of the Jerboa team, Noel, Tensingh, Gina and co are always unfailingly helpful in a myriad of ways and for that many thanks.

My eldest brother, Roy, has created a wonderful web site for me and is always extremely helpful with matters of research so huge thanks to him for all the ongoing work of many years.

Next I would like to thank all the children (and adults) who read my Djinn books and enjoy them and are kind enough to tell me so. It is for you (as well as to keep myself sane) that I write. Your enjoyment makes it all the more worthwhile. I hope Storm Djinn has kept or will keep you gripped and enthralled and reading under your duvet with a torch all night.

I took my inspiration for Storm Djinn from the Rub al Khali, the Empty Quarter, where I went with my family. We did a two day 'desert crossing' - a small incursion into the vastness of its sands but enough to provoke serious awe and respect. I thank my husband, Rupert Wise, for driving us manfully and safely up, over, round and down some seriously hair-raising dunes.

And, as has become a wonderful family habit, Rupert has read aloud two separate drafts of Storm Djinn to me and our children, Hugh, Tom and Lara. Hearing your own work read aloud is a great treat and the most useful and effective editing tool. My children by their direct, incisive comments and by their facial expressions reveal to me what works and what doesn't. Rupert bravely sallies forth with pithy and useful comments too. So huge thanks to you four for a collaborative creative process and for filling my life with love and joy and purpose.

Photo by Stu Williamson

Linda Davies read Politics, Philosophy and Economics at Oxford University and then worked for seven years as an investment banker in New York and London. She escaped banking to write novels. Her novels have been translated into over thirty languages. She lived for three years in Peru before returning to London. For the past five years she has lived with her husband, Rupert Wise, and their three children in Dubai.

She has just completed Storm Djinn, the third novel in her Djinn Quintet.